The Prince of Physics

Adventures in Reason

Kris Langman

Post Hoc Publishing

The Prince of Physics
Copyright © 2014 by Kris Langman
ISBN: 978-1520308333
Print Edition
Post Hoc Publishing

The purpose of the *Logic to the Rescue* series is to provide an introduction to logical fallacies and basic science. Neither the author nor Post Hoc Publishing assumes any liability with respect to loss or damage alleged to have been caused by the information in this book.

Chapter One

The Trackless Forest

"**M**ISS, WAKE UP!"

Nikki rolled over, blinking up at Athena, who was pulling off the woolen blankets covering Nikki and Curio.

"What is it?" asking Nikki, yawning widely as she sat up. "It can't be morning already. I just fell asleep." She glanced groggily around at the cave where they had spent the night. It was cool and peaceful, though Nikki thought she could hear faint voices shouting in the distance, down one of the tunnels leading from the cave.

"No, Miss. It is not morning," said the imp, wringing her tiny hands. "It is an attack. The Warning Bell has been sounded. We must flee."

Nikki's eyes widened and she sprang up, a little too hastily. Her head hit the low ceiling of the cave and shook loose a shower of dirt. Swearing under her breath, she brushed the dirt from her shoulders and lifted Curio to his feet. The tiny boy was just short enough to stand upright in the low cave.

"Wassamatter?" he mumbled, swaying back and forth with his eyes still closed.

Nikki gave him a little shake. "C'mon, Curio, wake up. Athena says we have to go."

"HaveGoWhere?" said Curio, trying to lie down again.

"Yes," said Nikki, turning to Athena, "go where, exactly? Who's attacking? Is it Fortuna and her Lurkers?"

"No, Miss," said Athena, hurriedly stuffing things into a leather pouch she had tied to her waist. "It is the Knights of the Iron Fist. Our watchers who guard the perimeter of our headquarters have spread the word that the Knights are surrounding us from all sides. How they found us, I don't know. This place is known only to imps. Fortunately, the Knights are too big to get into the tunnels. But that won't save us. They are lighting fires at all the tunnel entrances to drive us out with the smoke." She lit a beeswax candle from a torch on the wall of the cave. "This way, Miss. Hurry."

Nikki grabbed her rucksack, stuffed a squirming Cation into its depths and threw it over her shoulder. "But what about Fuzz and Gwen?" she asked as she herded Curio into the tunnel and ducked down to follow.

"They are already awake," said Athena over her shoulder. "They are helping with the evacuation. We have many escape routes in place. Most of us should be able to avoid capture. We can move through the forest much faster than bulky knights, with all their armor and horses."

They hurried down the tunnel as fast as they could, Athena pausing at intervals to wait for Curio and Nikki to catch up. Unlike the imp they were hampered by their height, and soon had to resort to crawling along on their hands and knees.

"What will the Knights do to us and to the other imps if they catch us?" asked Nikki, wincing as a stone cut into her knee. They had been crawling for what seemed like hours, going deeper and deeper into the complex, occasionally branching into a side tunnel, but mostly going in the same downhill direction.

"I am not sure, Miss," said Athena. "I think it is unlikely they will harm us. These are the same knights who charged Confounded Castle, trying to fight the sorcerer who was tormenting the people of the Haunted Hills. Remember when they escorted us from the inn and left us at the border of the Haunted Hills? They did not hurt us. In fact, they seemed almost embarrassed by their role in the matter."

"Yeah, but they still did it," said Nikki. "On Rufius's orders."

"Yes, Miss," said Athena. "They do seem to be in league with that very clean but very nasty young man. It is most unfortunate, as the Knights are a large order with many members. They have castles and fortresses all over the Realm. They are supposed to be loyal to the King, but I am having my doubts about that. I will make sure his Majesty learns of this attack. He will give the Knights a stern talking-to. He will not allow this kind of thuggery in his Realm." The imp halted, blowing out her candle. "We are near an exit, Miss. I will go ahead. Wait here."

Nikki was about to protest, but Athena had already disappeared. Nikki sank to a sitting position, leaning against the dirt wall of the tunnel. Cation poked her head out from under the flap of the rucksack and tickled Nikki's neck with her whiskers. Nikki scratched her under the chin until the kitten sank back down into the rucksack, purring.

Curio crossed his scrawny arms, his breath coming in little nervous whistles through his missing front teeth. "Quite a spot we've got ourselves into, isn't it Miss?" he said. "Almost makes me wish I was back in D-ville selling Hyperbolic Tonic."

"It's going to be okay," said Nikki with more confidence than she felt. The Realm of Reason seemed to be heading into chaos, maybe even civil war. Athena kept saying that the King would fix everything and restore peace in the land, but how could such a lazy, pleasure-loving monarch stand up to ruthless people like Fortuna, Maleficious and Rufius? Nikki sighed. Politics was not something she knew much about. At home it was something that the grown-ups in her life had dealt with. She had just studied hard and mostly ignored world events. But here in the Realm she had been thrust into a grown-up role she wasn't sure she was ready for.

Stones rattled in the tunnel. Nikki and Curio shrank against the tunnel wall and held their breath.

"It is just me, Miss," whispered Athena. "I have been to the entrance of this tunnel. There is no one about. This entrance is deep within the Trackless Forest, and it is well hidden by bushes and brambles. They knights have not found it. Follow me. Quickly."

They emerged into a night almost as dark as the inside of the tunnel. Wind whistled in the branches of towering fir trees and the ground was soft and mossy underfoot. An owl hooted high up in the trees. Athena led them deep into the forest, far away from the headquarters of the imps. Occasionally they followed meandering tracks which Athena said were made by deer, but mostly they had no path to follow. Nikki wondered how Athena could tell which way to go. The miles of trees looked completely the same to her in all directions, with no landmarks at all. No river or stream to follow, no high mountains to aim for. Nikki knew how easy it was to get lost in a forest. Her Mom had taken her on an Orienteering course once in the forests of the Wisconsin Dells. The course required them to find certain spots in the forest using a compass and a topographic map which showed the contours and elevations of the forest in great detail. Even with the compass and map they'd gotten lost several times. Here in the Trackless Forest Athena seemed to be navigating by some mysterious instinct. Nikki followed the imp worriedly. She hoped Athena knew what she was doing. It would be easy to get lost, wandering around in circles until they became weak from lack of food.

After walking through sunrise, high noon, and sunset the imp finally stopped.

"We will rest here for a bit, Miss." Athena handed them each a piece of cheese from the pouch around her waist.

Nikki plopped down on the ground and put her back against the rough bark of a fir tree while she munched on the cheese. The mossy ground was cold and wet and a breeze chilled the top of her head. Nikki pulled up the hood of her woolen tunic. Cation poked her head out of the rucksack and Nikki fed her a piece of cheese. Darkness was falling and she could just make out Athena and Curio sitting across from her on a fallen log, both of them shivering with cold. "I don't hear anyone," she said after listening intently for a moment. "Not knights or imps. Do you think the knights will follow us this far into the forest?"

"It is unlikely, Miss," said Athena, smoothing her gray dress. "They are no match for us imps in a forest and they know it. They are used to riding along on smooth roads on their horses. There are no roads through the Trackless Forest. Most likely the Knights will retreat back to their castles in the Haunted Hills."

"What about the other imps that were at the headquarters?" asked Nikki. "Are they all wandering around this forest like we are?"

"We are not wandering around, Miss," said Athena, a slightly hurt tone in her voice. "I have been in the Trackless Forest many times, beginning when I was a young girl. My grandmother used to take me to visit the Hermits. They have a small encampment about two days walk from here, deep in the forest. They don't like visitors, but they know me. I believe they will let us stay with them for a day or two, not more. They are very unsociable. But they have a spring of clean water and stores of food, which we will need. This cheese is all that I was able to pack."

"Will Fuzz and Gwen head for this hermit camp?" asked Nikki.

Athena shook her head. "Fuzz has never been there. He does not know this forest well. There are no taverns here for his gamblings and his beer guzzlings." She sniffed. "Fuzz has his uses in a large, dirty, smelly city like Deceptionville. He is better at all the bribing and lying and corrupt practices than I am. But he is not an experienced woodsman." She picked up a stick and drew a line in the dirt, then another line perpendicular to it. She marked the vertical line with an

'N'. "The hermit camp is almost directly north of our headquarters, Miss. When the sun rose in the east this morning I was careful to keep it on our right-hand side. Once the sun was directly overhead I knew it was noon and that it would start to sink over to the west. So I then kept the sun on our left-hand side. This kept us going in a roughly northern direction." She pointed up at the sky, where a patch of bright stars shone through the waving fir branches. "Now that it is getting dark I can navigate by the Warrior's Belt, Miss. It is those three bright stars arranged in a line like a belt. I can tell whether we are headed in a northerly direction by the angle these stars make with the horizon. It is more difficult to do this in a forest, with all the trees blocking the horizon, but it is not impossible. This type of star navigation was taught to me by my grandmother. Fuzz does not know how to do this. I believe he will try to stay along the edge of the forest, possibly doubling back toward the Haunted Hills. He will not risk getting lost in the Trackless Forest. Hopefully Miss Gwendolyn is with him."

Nikki's heart sank. No doubt Athena's woodland skills were excellent, but it was unnerving travelling with just Athena and Curio for companions. No matter how streetwise he was, Curio was still just a small boy. And while Athena was very capable, she didn't have Fuzz's talent for getting out of tight spots. If it hadn't been for Fuzz she and Athena would still be locked in the dungeon of Castle Cogent. And Gwen's talents for engineering, chemistry, and physics would come in very handy if they had to defend themselves from the Knights of the Iron Fist.

"After we have refreshed our food supplies at the hermit camp we will head for the Southern Castle," said Athena. "The King is there. He always stays there this time of year. And he brings many of his most trusted advisors with him. They will know how to deal with the problem of the Knights. Fuzz will head to the Southern Castle also, though it may take him longer as he will have to go around the Trackless Forest."

Chapter Two

◆●◆

The Hermit Camp

NIKKI SLID CURIO off of her back and laid him gently on the ground. They had been walking for two days without food and all three of them were weak. Curio had stubbornly trudged along behind them, but by the middle of the second day he had reached the end of his strength. Nikki felt wobbly from hunger herself, but she had started giving Curio piggy-back rides. After the first day of their journey the forest changed from tall firs with mossy ground which was easy to walk on to a mix of pines and alders with a tangled undergrowth of rhododendron bushes. Curio's weight on her back made plowing through the thick undergrowth exhausting. When Athena had finally called a halt Nikki felt like she could sleep for a week.

Nikki lay down on the ground next to Curio and closed her eyes.

They were in a grassy clearing near the hermit camp. Athena had told them to wait while she went ahead to warn the hermits of their arrival. Apparently they didn't take kindly to unexpected visitors. Bees buzzed in the wildflowers dotting the clearing and overhead in a pine tree a Blue Jay cawed. It was pleasant lying there in the sun, the warm grass soothing her tired muscles. Nikki dozed off.

"Miss!" said Athena, shaking Nikki's shoulder. "Wake up please. Prospero has agreed to let us stay at the camp for three days. It is very generous of him."

"Who?" asked Nikki groggily. She rolled over and stumbled to her feet. Her rucksack slid off her shoulder and a rumpled Cation tumbled out onto the grass, shaking each tiny furry foot and yawning widely. The kitten sniffed warily at a nearby bluebell and hissed when a bee flew out of it and buzzed her nose.

"Ah, a sprite in feline form! How felicitous!"

"What's a sprite?" asked Curio, sitting up and rubbing his eyes.

"A sprite is a pint-sized goddess, young sir," said the hermit Athena introduced as Prospero. He was an elderly man with long white hair sprouting from his chin and out of each ear. The only place hair wasn't sprouting was from the top of his head, which was as smooth and bald as a newly-laid egg. He wore a rough brown woolen robe tied at the waist with a piece of rope. The robe had burn marks all over it and gave off a distinct smell of sulfur. Nikki wondered if he was inclined to experiment with chemicals the same way Gwen was.

"I have a feline companion myself," continued the hermit, bending down and holding out a small piece of meat to Cation. "Her name is Per and she is a sly one, with silky black fur and green eyes that can see into a man's soul."

The kitten approached cautiously, sniffing first at the hem of Prospero's robe before suddenly seizing the meat in her mouth and dashing behind Nikki. She settled into the grass and chewed away happily, her purring harmonizing with the buzzing of the bees.

"A cautious one, she is" said the hermit approvingly. "Can't be too careful where strangers are concerned." He gave Nikki and Curio a meaningful stare.

Athena frowned. "Prospero, these are friends of mine, as I have already told you. I am the king's emissary, as you well know, and these two are helping me on an errand for the king."

Prospero waved a knobby hand. "King, Shming. I have no use for earthly monarchs. The only authorities I bow to are the heavenly ones." He raised his arms skyward and closed his eyes in rapture.

"Venus, that capricious goddess, her light glowing low in the heavens both morning and evening, bringing good luck or bad to us puny humans, depending on her whims. Mars, that mighty god of power and war, bringing pestilence and plague when he burns red with anger at our misdeeds."

Nikki rolled her eyes. Astrology was apparently as popular here in the Realm as it was in her world. How people could think that planets millions of miles away from them could possibly have any effect on human affairs was something she had never understood. Apparently some people thought that everything in the universe affected them personally. As she watched Prospero swaying back and forth, a goofy grin on his face, she was suddenly struck by the fact that he had called the planets by the same names used in her world. Venus and Mars.

When they had been camping on the riverbank back in Deceptionville she had studied the night sky, trying to find any familiar constellations: the Big Dipper, Ursa Major, Orion. She hadn't found any. But now it seemed that her world and the Realm shared the same planets in the night sky, which must mean that they were in the same solar system. The fact that they used exactly the same names for the planets was even more startling. And now that she thought about it, how was it possible for her to understand people in this world at all? Were they speaking English? Nikki's mouth dropped open in surprise, feeling stupid that she hadn't noticed this before. She looked warily around at the grassy clearing, feeling dizzy and disoriented, the same way she'd felt when she'd been all alone in the tower of the Confounded Castle. Where exactly was she? Fuzzy thoughts about parallel universes and portals and hallucinations and two Nikkis, one here in the Realm and one back home at the Wisconsin State High School Debate Championships flashed through her mind. She felt dizzier and dizzier, wondering if she was going to throw up. She sat down abruptly, narrowly missing Cation, who growled and dragged her half-eaten piece of meat away to the safety of a nearby rhododendron bush.

"Miss, are you all right?" asked Athena, kneeling down next to Nikki and looking at her worriedly.

Nikki nodded. "Just hungry," she said, trying to pull herself together. Wherever she was, she couldn't afford to fall apart. She pushed her confusing thoughts about the Realm and its location in the universe to the back of her mind. There was a time and place for deep thinking and this was not it. Back to practical matters. Nikki took a deep breath and rose shakily to her feet.

Athena patted her hand. "Now, Prospero. These children need nourishment. At once."

The hermit was still swaying back and forth, humming softly to himself, his eyes closed.

Sparks flashed in Athena's eyes. She marched up to Prospero, grabbed a handful of his long white beard, and gave it a hard yank.

"Owww!" yelped the hermit.

Athena wagged a finger at him. "It's no more than you deserve, with your swayings and mumblings. Wasting time while these children starve. Take us to your food supplies. This instant."

Prospero led the way out of the clearing, grumbling under his breath and rubbing his chin.

They followed him along a well-worn path bordering a rushing stream. Cation raced ahead, chasing a chipmunk which had skittered down from a tall pine tree. Every few feet the chipmunk would skid to halt, looking back over its shoulder as if daring the kitten to come and get it. Cation would crouch down, a growl low in her throat, and suddenly bound forward. But before she could sink her claws into its fur the chipmunk would dash away again, emitting a high-pitched squeak which sounded suspiciously like giggling.

Prospero roared with laughter. "The feline sprite has met her match! The forest has its own mischievous sprites. This striped-back little fellow is harmless, but she should be on her guard. Not all of the demons lurking in the forest are innocent pranksters. Not far from here is the nest of a horned owl infested with a Nightmare demon. When it swoops overhead your dreams become filled with the most vile imaginings. Especially if you've been partaking of Brother Melvin's honey and lavender mead."

Athena sighed. "There are no demons in this forest, Prospero. Or in any other forest. There are just owls and chipmunks and silly hermits who should know better than to drink mead. Stop filling the children's heads with nonsense."

Prospero chuckled good-naturedly. "You always were a hard-headed little walnut, my dear Athena. Never willing to admit that there might be invisible forces in the world. Things which your eyes can't see."

"There are many invisible things which my eyes cannot see," said Athena. "The wind, the heat of a fire, a raindrop at the bottom of a river. Yet these things are real, as I am perfectly willing to admit. They affect the real world in ways which can be verified. But these demons of yours are just figments of your overactive imagination, Prospero. You and Fuzz are two of a kind. Him with his ghosts and you with your demons. You both never stop to ask yourselves if the things in your head actually exist in the real world."

Prospero shrugged. "The real world is often disappointing, Athena my dear. Some of us prefer to live in a world of pleasant thoughts rather than a world of harsh realities." He stopped on the path and held out his arms. "Behold our humble encampment. I'm afraid we can't provide the luxuries of the king's castle, but you should be comfortable here for a few days."

Nikki came up next to Athena and peered around at the wide clearing in the forest. The hermit camp was bigger than she had imagined. Near where they stood was a well made out of rough stones. Water bubbled over its mossy lip and into a rock-lined ditch which cut the clearing in two. On either side of this man-made stream clustered a motley group of dwellings. Some were simple canvas tents, others were piles of igloo-shaped stones, a few were small wooden buildings which reminded her of log cabins. At the far end of the clearing was a large pen holding a cow and a few sheep. Goats roamed here and there, chewing on the grass and weeds like four-legged lawnmowers. The clearing smelled of wood smoke and goat poop.

Prospero beckoned them on and they followed him across the goat-manicured grass. They had only gone a few steps when a huge black dog, taller than Curio, dashed up and barked at them furiously, its whole body trembling with rage at this intrusion on its territory. Curio turned white and slid behind Nikki, who had frozen in place. Cation hissed and scrambled up Nikki's pant leg, her tiny claws digging painfully into Nikki's flesh. Nikki grabbed her and stuffed the kitten into her rucksack.

Athena put one hand on her hip and wagged a finger at the dog. "Bad Caliban! Don't you recognize friends when you see them?" She held out a tiny hand for the dog to sniff.

Nikki held her breath. The dog was big enough to gobble down Athena in a few bites.

It growled deep in its throat and padded up to the imp on paws the size of a horse's hooves. It sniffed suspiciously at Athena's hand and the hem of her dress. Some scent memory seemed to calm it, for it suddenly plopped down on its haunches and hung its head, as if ashamed of the greeting it had given them.

Athena smiled and scratched its head. "Caliban is Benedict's dog, so I assume he is still with you. The last time I was here Benedict told me he was leaving your camp to travel the wide world."

Prospero sniffed. "Benedict says a lot of things which don't come to pass. He lasted only a week in the wide world, as you call it. It turned out to be a little too wide for him. He only made it as far as the Haunted Hills before he ran back here like a lost child. I gather that people in the wide world expected him to earn his keep, a concept which Benedict has never managed to grasp. He's supposed to be tending our beehives right now, but I suspect he's abandoned the bees for his usual daydreaming." He frowned down at the black dog. "I don't mind Benedict coming back to us, but I wish he had left this mongrel in the Haunted Hills. The lumbering brute is constantly harassing my Per, my lovely feline goddess. It disturbs her delicate sensibilities to have this monster slobbering on her." He waved a dismissive hand at the dog, which gave Athena a final sniff and loped off into the trees. "The silly canine is a good watch dog, I'll say that much for him. We had a lost shepherd wander into our camp last month, and Caliban barked loud enough to raise the dead."

Athena raised her eyebrows. "A lost shepherd? Are you sure that's what he was? Your camp is a long way from the nearest sheep farm. More than three days march."

Prospero shrugged. "He said he was a shepherd. I had no reason to doubt him. He certainly smelled of sheep. We fed him, gave him a cot for two nights, and then one of our younger members led him back to the edge of the Haunted Hills. We were glad to be rid of him. He was a talkative young chap, constantly asking questions."

Athena looked up at him sharply. "What kind of questions?"

Prospero tugged thoughtfully on his beard. "He wanted to know if we'd had any visitors lately. Any imp visitors, especially. I told him no. You, Athena my dear, are the only imp which ever visits our humble camp."

"Did you tell him that I sometimes come here?" asked Athena.

Prospero shook his head. "No, I don't think so. The youngster was ill-mannered, and I wasn't inclined to chat much with him. You might ask Benedict. He spent more time in the shepherd's company. Now, let's get you settled in. We have an empty tent you can use. One of our newer members decided our isolated location wasn't to his liking and he took off for the coast, leaving his tent behind."

They followed Prospero to a tent at the far edge of the clearing. Its canvas sides brushed up against the pine trees which surrounded the camp. The grass in front of the tent had been stamped down and a stone fire-ring built. A small iron pot was sitting in its cold ashes and a pile of firewood was stacked nearby. A circle of logs made a makeshift bench surrounding the fire-ring.

Nikki pulled aside the tent flap and peeked inside. It was empty except for two cots made out of rough-hewn birch logs with canvas stretched between them. A pile of musty looking wool blankets had been dumped on one of the cots.

"Make yourselves at home," said Prospero. "I expect you'll want to rest after your journey. I will see about getting you some food." He wandered off toward one of the larger wooden buildings near the man-made stream.

Athena bustled about, shaking out the woolen blankets and picking miniscule pieces of dirt off them. She neatly folded two of the blankets and laid them on the cots, then made a little nest with the others in one corner of the tent.

"I think this will do for you," she said, beckoning to Curio. "Come and try it out."

Curio snuggled down into the blankets and yawned widely. "Yes, Miss, this is lovely. Much more comfortable than sleeping on the floor of my master's shop back in D-ville. If you'll excuse me, I think I'll just . . ."

Athena tiptoed out of the tent and left Curio to his nap.

Nikki took off her rucksack and put it on one of the cots. Cation scrambled out and looked around with a bewildered air.

Nikki smoothed her rumpled fur. "Must be confusing," she said. "Getting carted around in a sack and transported to unfamiliar places." She picked up the kitten and placed her next to Curio on the pile of blankets.

Cation yawned widely and kneaded Curio's stomach with her tiny paws. Once she'd ensured that the sleeping arrangements were to her liking she curled up into a ball and fell fast asleep.

Nikki quietly left the tent and took a seat on the logs next to Athena. Her stomach growled loudly.

Athena patted her hand. "Not much longer, Miss. See? Benedict is bringing us our lunch." She pointed at a young man who was hurrying across the clearing toward them. He was carrying a large wicker basket.

"Athena!" he yelled from fifty yards away. He waved at them enthusiastically, nearly dropping the basket.

Nikki studied him as he approached. He was much younger than Prospero, not much more than twenty, she guessed. To her mind he didn't look like a hermit at all. Prospero, with his long white beard and rough brown robe was her idea of a hermit. By contrast, Benedict was a bundle of glowing youth and energy. His blond hair shone in the sun and his spotless white tunic reminded her unpleasantly of Rufius. People who managed to keep their clothes clean always raised her suspicions. In her experience, people who worked hard and accomplished a lot tended to have stains and rips in their clothing. They were usually too busy to spend a lot of time on their appearance. Gwen was a perfect example, with her apron full of burns from her experiments with chemistry and metal-working. Nikki's mother was another example. She was always spilling things on herself. The white coats she wore in her chemistry lab were spotted all over with mysterious stains. Nikki once dared her to keep a new lab coat spot-free for an entire week, but her mother lost the dare after only one day.

Nikki sighed. Thinking about her mother made her feel both sad and a little guilty. She missed her Mom, but maybe not as much as she should. Events in the Realm of Reason had kept her very busy from the moment Athena and Fuzz had led her through the old boiler in the janitor's closet at her high school. She hadn't had much time to think about home, or about her Mom. She reminded herself of what the King had said at Castle Cogent, that no time would pass back home in Wisconsin while she was here in the Realm. Her Mom wouldn't even know she was gone. Still, it wouldn't do to completely forget everyone back home. She promised herself she'd spend a few minutes each day thinking about her Mom, her friends at school, and her debate teammates.

"Benedict, you careless boy. Give me that basket before you spill our lunch all over the grass." Athena bustled up to the young man and confiscated the basket. She lugged it to the fire-ring and set it carefully down.

"Now, let us see," she said, peering inside. "Bread, honey, cheese, jam. Not bad. A respectable repast. I am glad to see your camp has improved on its generosity to visitors. The last time I was here I was barely able to get a piece of dry bread."

Benedict plopped down onto a log next to the fire-ring and stretched out his legs.

Nikki stifled a giggle. His informality reminded her of the way the dog Caliban had flopped down at Athena's feet.

"The credit has to go to Prospero," said Benedict, flicking a piece of mud from his sandals. "He has tightened up our farming practices since last you visited. He has us working like industrious bees, from morning to night. Plowing, tilling, planting, harvesting, and gathering. I suppose it is all worth it, as we eat much better than we used to. But I have never worked so hard in my life. I feel like I'm back at my father's farm, tilling the fields like a slave. I left my boyhood home because of the back-breaking labor, and now I find myself right back where I started. It is much different from the life of quiet contempla-tion I had imagined."

Athena raised an eyebrow, running a skeptical eye over his white tunic. "You do not look like any farmhand I have ever seen, Benedict. You look more like the lazy courtiers at the king's court, who spend too much coin on silk tunics and embroidered cloaks and never work a day in their lives."

Benedict smiled good-naturedly. "I assure you, dear Athena, that I work like a plow horse every day. Old Prospero sees to it. He cracks the whip over me every hour of every day. I never get a minute of peace for my meditations. But I suppose it is all for the best. The universe must have a purpose in making Prospero work me so hard. After all, everything happens for a reason."

Nikki winced. Everything happens for a reason. She hated that phrase. She heard it at her school all the time, usually from kids who were heavily into astrology, Tarot cards, and other kinds of mystical nonsense. They seemed to have the bizarre idea that the universe was constantly watching them, as if they were the star of an imaginary Broadway play and there was an invisible audience applauding their every move. Even Tina, the captain of her debate team and someone who should have known better, was fond of saying it. Nikki had once gotten into a huge argument with Tina over it. They'd had a furious debate right in the school cafeteria, ignoring their tuna fish sandwiches while Tina's pack clapped at everything Tina said and booed every time Nikki opened her mouth.

"Everything most definitely does *not* happen for a reason," said Nikki, unable to resist commenting. "Most things which happen in life are random. There's no invisible scorekeeper pulling on unseen strings to make each event in your life turn out for the best."

Benedict stared at her, his mouth hanging open in astonishment.

Athena chuckled and handed them each a hunk of brown bread with a thick piece of cheese on top. "Though only a child she is far wiser than you, Benedict, for all your meditations. Thinking the world constantly provides reasons for everything that happens to you is pure egotism."

Benedict pouted, giving his open and friendly face the look of a spoiled child. "That's a bit harsh, Athena. People who know me would say that I'm the last person to be described as egotistical. If I were egotistical I certainly wouldn't be hiding out here in the wilderness, far from civilization. An egotistical person would be preening at the king's court, wearing those silks and embroideries you so despise."

Athena pulled a water jug out of the wicker basket and handed it to Nikki. "There are different kinds of egotism, Benedict. I do not accuse you of the obvious kind, the incessant need for attention which preeners have. But thinking that the universe is so obsessed with your doings that it comes up with reasons for every little happening in your daily life is another type of egotism. The universe is large, and you are small, Benedict. You are not at its center."

Nikki nodded in agreement. She was tempted to jump in with her billions of galaxies argument, the one she had used in her lunchtime debate with Tina. The astronomer Edwin Hubble had discovered in the 1920's that there were far more galaxies in the universe than just the Milky Way galaxy. And that each of those galaxies contained billions of stars. And in the 1990's other astronomers had proven that the stars in those distant galaxies had planets revolving around them. Trillions of worlds where life might potentially evolve. The idea that such a vast universe was obsessed with the daily doings of Tina, the sixteen-year-old debate team captain at Westlake High School, was ridiculous. And the same could be said for the daily doings of Benedict, hermit and denizen of the Trackless Forest in the Realm of Reason.

Nikki bit her lip to stop herself from speaking. Thinking about Edwin Hubble and his reflecting telescope on Mount Wilson in California had reminded her that the technology in her world was far ahead of what existed in the Realm of Reason. The Realm was centuries behind her world, its technology at a level somewhere around the time of Galileo. That was four hundred years ago. Long before the industrial revolution in her world had created things like the steam engine, trains, electricity, television, and telescopes large enough to see other galaxies. She felt like an anthropologist studying the ways of a tribe living in the depths of the Amazon jungle. How were her actions affecting this culture? Did she have the right to bring new ideas to the Realm? Would these new ideas disrupt things here? Were the people of the Realm ready for them? Nikki couldn't help feeling it would be dangerous to introduce them to ideas so different from what they were used to. It seemed better to let them eventually get to these ideas on their own, probably several centuries from now.

But, thinking back over the last few weeks she had spent in the Realm, there were already many times when she had spread new ideas. She had mentioned extractor fans to Gwen when Gwen had showed her the laboratory in the basement of Muddled Manor. And she had explained the basics of the atom to Curio when they were in the shop owned by Avaricious in Deceptionville. And she had mentioned nuclear reactors and particle accelerators to Avaricious himself, when he had insisted that gold could be created from lead. If there was anyone who should not be told about new technology, especially potentially harmful technology, it was Avaricious. Nikki shuddered at the damage he could do, which brought back her worries about Gwen's gunpowder experiment. She wondered if the Lurker who had seen the experiment had ever reported it to Avaricious or Fortuna or Rufius.

"Miss, you are very quiet," said Athena. "And you are not eating. Are you ill?"

Nikki blinked. Athena and Benedict were both staring at her. "No, I'm fine," she said quickly. "I was just thinking about Gwen. I hope she's okay."

"I am sure Miss Gwendolyn is fine," said Athena. "Fuzz will see that no harm comes to her. He is a beer-guzzling rascal, but he knows how to avoid trouble when he wants to. You will see, they will be at the Southern Castle, waiting for us."

Benedict's eyes widened. "You're travelling to the Southern Castle? Oh, Athena take me with you! You have no idea how I long to escape from the drudgery which is my lot in life."

Nikki swallowed a giggle at Benedict's melodramatic outburst.

Athena wasn't laughing. She glared at the young hermit. "Your place is here, Benedict. Prospero needs youngsters like you to keep this camp going. Most of the hermits here are growing too old to till the fields, and they have always had difficulties in getting new recruits. Young people don't like being out here in the wilderness. They prefer the attractions and temptations of large cities like Deceptionville." The imp sniffed, as if she could smell the dirty alleys of Deceptionville from way out here in the Trackless Forest.

Nikki grinned. Athena reminded her of the stiff-necked Puritans she had studied in her history class at school. The imp had the same judgmental attitude toward pleasures, both harmless ones and destructive ones, as those early settlers in New England. But she admired Athena's backbone. The little imp was a tower of strength and fortitude, despite her size. Nikki wished she had met more imps in her travels through the Realm. Athena and Fuzz were the only ones she had talked to so far. She'd seen other imps at a distance, in Popularnum and in Deceptionville, but she hadn't spoken with any of them. She wondered if they were somehow different from humans. Judging by Athena and Fuzz, the only difference was their size. Nikki glanced around the wide, grassy clearing of the hermit camp. The only people she could see were normal-sized humans, all of them male, most of them elderly. No imps.

The imp headquarters. That would have been the place to meet imps. Unfortunately they'd been chased from there by the Knights of the Iron Fist before she'd had a chance to meet any of the inhabitants. She absentmindedly took a bite of bread and cheese and wondered where all the imps had scattered to. Were they all headed for the Southern Castle? She was just about to ask Athena when a horrible scream, full of pain and terror, erupted from the center of the camp.

Nikki dropped the piece of bread she was holding and jumped up. Athena and Benedict were already racing toward the sound, the tiny imp straining to keep up with Benedict's long strides. Nikki ran after them, catching up just as they came to a skidding halt in front of a wooden cabin.

A crowd of old men was gathered in front of the cabin, staring at something on the ground.

Nikki peered around the shoulder of a tall hermit with black hair and a gray woolen robe. Lying on the ground was a painfully thin young man dressed in a torn robe. His arms and legs looked like skin-covered sticks, and saliva was dribbling from his mouth. He thrashed back and forth, beating his hands on the ground. His whole body was shaking as if a powerful electric current was passing through it. His back arched away from the ground as if he were trying to do a backbend.

An epileptic fit. Nikki was sure of it. A girl at her high school suffered from epilepsy and Nikki had once seen the girl have a seizure in the parking lot. Her symptoms had been almost exactly the same as this. The arched back, the shaking, the thrashing arms and legs. And . . . Nikki gasped, the blue tinge in her face. This young man was also turning blue.

"He's choking!" she shouted. "He can't breathe!"

When no one moved Nikki tried to push past the tall hermit to get to the young man on the ground.

"Hold up there, girl," said the tall hermit, grabbing her arm. "You don't want to get too close. The demon might just decide to leave Brother Jonathan and hop into you. And it's a nasty one. For years now it's tortured poor Jonathan something awful."

Nikki tried to shake off his hand but he held her fast. "It's not a demon," she said, "it's a seizure. I've seen it before." She turned to Athena in desperation. "This type of seizure leaves him with no control over his muscles. Including the muscles of his tongue. He's choking. He can't breathe. Athena, please. I know what to do."

Athena looked up at her doubtfully. "I know you want to help, Miss, but there is no telling what he might do in his condition. He might hit or even bite you."

"Benedict can hold him down," said Nikki. "Now tell this man to let go of me. We're running out of time."

Benedict looked rather alarmed at being conscripted into service, but he dutifully stepped forward and knelt down by the shaking man.

Athena gestured to the tall hermit to let Nikki go.

Nikki dashed forward and knelt near the young man's head. "Hold his arms down," she said.

Benedict nodded and forced the man's jerking arms down onto the ground.

Nikki tilted the man's head back to check his airway. As she'd suspected, he had vomited and his airway was blocked. "Turn him on his side," she said to Benedict.

Benedict rolled him onto his side, still holding his jerking arms. A rush of vomit flowed out of the young man's mouth and pooled on the ground. His thin chest expanded as he took great gulps of air and the blue color started to fade from his face.

Nikki breathed a sigh of relief. She knelt by him until the shaking stopped.

Benedict let go of his arms and the young man collapsed into what looked like a deep sleep.

Nikki put a hand on his chest. It was rising and falling with his breath. He was out of danger. She got shakily to her feet.

Athena took her hand and patted it. "Well done, Miss. Well done."

A buzz of muttered comments came from the hermits.

To her surprise Nikki noticed that they were all looking at her suspiciously.

Finally the tall hermit who had grabbed her spoke. "How did you make the demon leave him, girl? Did you take the demon into yourself?"

The circle of hermits took a step back from her, their glances changing from suspicion to fear.

"What? No, of course not," said Nikki. "There never *was* any demon. He was having a seizure. I've seen them before." She frantically searched her memory for any facts about epilepsy. She didn't know much about it. "It has something to do with electrical activity in the brain. An electrical storm, I think they call it. Electricity is kind of like lightning. Think of tiny little lightning bolts in your head. When someone has epilepsy these tiny little lightning bolts get too strong, and they send signals which are too strong to the person's muscles. That causes the shaking and the jerking of the person's arms and legs. I'm not explaining it very well. A doctor could explain it better."

"What is a doctor?" asked Benedict. He was the only hermit who was looking at Nikki with curiosity rather than fear.

"A doctor is someone who treats health problems," said Nikki. "If you have a broken leg, or a disease, you go to a doctor and they make you well again."

Benedict nodded. "Like a healer." He pointed at an elderly hermit who was leaning on a crude wooden crutch. "Brother Jerome is our healer here at the camp."

Brother Jerome hobbled forward, leaning heavily on his crutch. He was so short and bent that he only came up to Nikki's shoulder. His deeply lined face looked like a patch of mud that had baked in the sun and cracked into pieces. He straightened his crooked neck as much as he could and peered intently into Nikki's eyes.

"Yes, I can see it," he intoned in a deep, impressive voice. "The demon has left Brother Jonathan and is now residing in this young girl."

A gasp went up from the hermits.

Brother Jerome waved them to silence. "We must perform an exorcism on the girl. Force this foul demon to leave our camp once and for all."

The hair on the back of Nikki's neck stood up. She didn't like the sound of this at all. Her mother had never let her watch the movie *The Exorcist*, but she'd heard enough about it to know that she definitely didn't want anyone performing an exorcism on her. Apart from being stupid and pointless, it sounded dangerous. She backed away from the group of hermits. "Athena, talk to them. Whatever this exorcism stuff is, I don't want them doing it to me."

"No, of course not, Miss," said Athena. She stepped into the middle of the ring of hermits and wagged a tiny finger at them. "You are being noodle-heads. This exorcism nonsense must stop. I will not allow it."

"*You* will not allow it," sneered the tall, black-haired hermit. "You are not the leader here, imp."

Athena turned to face him, a cold look on her face. "My name is Athena, sir. Not Imp. And despite your rudeness you are correct. I am not the leader of this camp. Prospero is. Where is he? We will put this question of exorcism to him, and I am sure he will not allow it."

The tall hermit snorted. "He has allowed it thus far. Brother Jerome has performed the exorcism rituals on Brother Jonathan many times and Prospero has done nothing to stop it. He doesn't want demons in this camp any more than the rest of us do."

Athena sighed deeply. "Silly, silly hermits. There are no such things as demons. Demons, ghosts, these are stories to scare young children with. They are imaginings in the dark, when the wind howls and tree branches scratch against the roof. You need to stop and ask yourselves if you have ever actually seen a demon. Have you ever heard one? Have you ever smelled or touched one? They exist only as creatures in your head. Products of your imagination. You have failed to do the most basic, the most important test: have you taken this idea of demons and checked it against reality? No, you have not. If you had you would have seen that they do not exist in reality, but only in your minds."

The circle of hermits muttered angrily, glaring at Athena.

"Enough of this," said Brother Jerome. "Demons are everywhere, as any sensible person knows. The one which was residing in Brother Jonathan is especially evil. It has been tormenting him for years. Now that it has left him and jumped to this girl we may have a chance to rid ourselves of it for good." He gestured with a clawed hand at Nikki. "Bring her to the Lockhouse."

Nikki let out a startled shriek as the tall hermit suddenly grabbed her and swung her over his shoulder. He carried her across the grassy clearing with Brother Jerome hobbling after them on his crutch. Athena ran alongside the tall hermit, pummeling his legs with her tiny fists. He ignored her as if she was an annoying fly buzzing around him.

They came to a halt in front of a small wooden hut isolated from the other buildings.

Nikki had a brief glimpse of its windowless sides before the tall hermit carried her inside and dumped her on the dirt floor. He left, closing the heavy wooden door behind him. Nikki heard a thump as a bar was dropped in place across the door, locking her in. She picked herself up off the floor and threw her weight against the door, but it was no use. She was trapped.

Chapter Three

Two Alone

NIKKI COULD HEAR Athena arguing with the hermits, but the imp's voice was faint, muffled by the thick walls of the hut. She looked around the bare room. The front door was the only opening. No windows, no chimney, not even a shaft for air. The room was stuffy and smelled of the chamber pot which was shoved into a corner. Nikki slumped down on the dirt floor with her back against the door and tried not to panic.

She wondered if the young hermit with epilepsy had been locked in here. The stuffy, smelly air certainly couldn't have done him any good. She tried not to think about what might have been done to him in the hut.

The hermits didn't seem like bad people. Prospero was a bit goofy and detached from reality, but he seemed nice enough. He had generously offered them food and shelter without expecting anything in return. Benedict was friendly and curious, maybe a little lazy, but that wasn't a crime. She didn't care much for the healer, Brother Jerome, or the tall hermit whose name she didn't know, but even they had to be better than Fortuna and her Lurkers. Or greedy Avaricious, or power-hungry Rufius. The hermits were just frightened. The problem was, what they were frightened of didn't actually exist. That made the situation much more difficult than if they were frightened of something everyone could see, like a wolf invading their camp or a bear growling in the woods nearby.

Trying to prove that something didn't exist was extremely difficult. She guessed that Athena was outside trying to do just that: prove to the hermits that demons didn't exist. If demons didn't exist then there was no need for an exorcism and they could let her out of this nasty little hut.

Evidence of absence. That's what her debate teacher called it, and you didn't want to be stuck in the position of trying to prove evidence of absence in a debate. A big part of the problem was that you could never be sure something didn't exist. There were simply too many scenarios to run through. An infinite number of them. Especially when what you were trying to disprove was undetectable.

Like demons. Demons and similar imaginary things like ghosts were always conveniently invisible, untouchable, un-smellable. Someone who believed in invisible things was always careful to make the demon or ghost impossible to detect. Making it untestable, her teacher called it. If you suggested using an instrument such as an infrared detector to detect the heat given off by a demon, the believer would insist that demons had no body heat. If you suggested trying to detect the demon using a radio-wave receiver, the believer would insist that demons didn't give off radio waves. Even if the believer said that the demon made noises and you suggested recording the noise using a tape recorder, the believer would insist that demon-noise couldn't be recorded. This could go on forever, with the person on one side of the debate suggesting various demon-detection devices and the believer always insisting that the test didn't apply to their particular demon.

And here in the Realm they didn't have technology like radio-wave receivers or tape recorders anyway. Athena would have to convince the hermits that demons didn't exist using only logical arguments. Athena would say there was no proof that demons existed, but the hermits would just argue that there was no proof that they didn't. The hermits would be committing a logical fallacy called Appeal to Ignorance, which was used in debates to shift the burden of proof to the other debater, in this case to Athena. In both debating and in logical argument in general the person stating the existence of something had the burden of proving it. If you said demons existed you had to prove it. But a very common tactic of people with no good evidence for their belief was to claim that their opponent had to provide proof of the non-existence of their belief. The believers were committing a logical fallacy, but people listening to the debate or argument usually didn't notice. The Appeal to Ignorance was a tricky fallacy. You had to have a pretty strong understanding of logic to spot it. Most people just assumed that the believer and the non-believer were on equal ground, when in fact the burden of proof was always on the believer.

Nikki chewed nervously on a fingernail. Athena wasn't going to get her out of this exorcism using logic. The hermits were too insistent that demons were real and no amount of debate was going to change their minds.

Various types of rituals began running through her thoughts. Things she'd seen in movies or on TV. There was that PBS show she'd seen, where a shaman belonging to a Navajo tribe had blown cedar smoke over a woman to expel an evil spirit which was supposedly inside her. Smudging. That's what the show had called it. Burning sage plants or cedar twigs and fanning the smoke over a person. That didn't seem so bad. The worst it could do would be to give her a coughing fit. If she was given a choice about what type of exorcism she wanted she'd definitely vote for smudging. But somehow she didn't think the hermits were going to give her a choice.

Her history class at school had studied various tribal rituals, some of which had to do with expelling demons from a person. There was that ritual some West African tribes did, where they buried a live chicken under a banana tree. Pretty hard on the chicken, but if it came down to a choice between a chicken or herself, Nikki was okay with sacrificing the chicken.

She tried hard not to think about the Spanish Inquisition, which they'd also studied in history class. The Spanish priests had burned people at the stake, though she couldn't remember why. Nikki shuddered. Don't even go there, she told herself firmly. These hermits were friends of Athena. Or at least Prospero was. They wouldn't do anything as awful as burning her at the stake.

Her stomach growled loudly. She wished she'd eaten more than just a few bites of bread and cheese. The basket Benedict had brought them had been full to the brim with food. She should have eaten until she was full, but maybe it was better that she hadn't. After two days of tramping through the Trackless Forest without food her stomach was feeling weird. If she'd stuffed herself she probably would have been sick. Thinking about the basket of food reminded her that Curio was still napping in their tent with Cation. The cozy mental picture of the two of them curled up together made her feel a bit better. She curled up into a ball on the dirt floor and fell asleep dreaming about Cation chasing the chipmunk along the path to the hermit camp. Brother Jerome appeared, hobbling along on his crutch. He snatched up the chipmunk by the tail and declared it possessed by a chipmunk-demon. Nikki jerked awake just as Brother Jerome was lowering the chipmunk into a pot of boiling water.

"Miss! Miss! Are you in there?"

Nikki scrambled to her feet and put her ear to the door. The voice was very hard to hear. The walls of the hut were thick and the speaker was whispering.

"Athena?" she whispered back.

"No, Miss. It's me."

"Curio? What are you doing? Where's Athena?"

"She's still arguing with the hermits, Miss. It's not going well."

A rasping sound came from the other side of the door.

"Curio, what are you doing? I don't want you to get in trouble. I don't trust some of these hermits."

"Me neither, Miss. That tall one reminds me of a Deceptionville Rounder. A bully, he is. I've seen my share of them."

There was a bump against the door and Curio grunted loudly.

"Almost had it, Miss. It's very heavy, this bar across the door."

He grunted again and suddenly gave a loud yelp.

"Curio! What's wrong?"

There was no answer.

Nikki jumped back as the door suddenly swung inward. A tall figure stood in the doorway, beckoning to her.

"Benedict!" exclaimed Nikki.

The young hermit put a finger to his lips and urgently waved her forward.

Nikki didn't have to be asked twice. She darted out of the hut, nearly bowling over Curio, who was just behind Benedict. He jumped up and down with joy.

"You're free, Miss!"

"Not yet, young sir," whispered Benedict. "You need to leave the camp at once. Brother Jerome is stirring up the others against you. He doesn't like outsiders and resents your presence here."

"We can't leave without Athena," said Nikki.

"I will invent some excuse to talk to her and lead her away from the others," said Benedict. "In the meantime you two must hide in the forest. Follow me, quickly."

"Cation!" whispered Nikki. "I'm not leaving without her."

"Here she is, Miss," said Curio, holding out Nikki's rucksack, which was purring.

Nikki grinned and shouldered the pack, which kept on purring.

"This way," said Benedict.

They followed him across the grassy clearing. The sun had set and it was very dark, with no moon. The fires glowing in front of tents and cabins didn't provide enough light to see by. Nikki's feet slid on the dew-dampened grass. The smell of meat roasting somewhere made her stomach growl. She hoped Benedict was going to provide them with food before they made their escape.

They had almost made it to the edge of the clearing when a tall figure suddenly stepped out of a nearby cabin.

"Benedict! Where are you going? You should be helping to prepare the evening meal."

It was the tall hermit who had locked Nikki in the hut.

Nikki and Curio ducked behind Benedict.

"Um, Brother Jerome has requested blackberries in honey for his meal," said Benedict, his voice quavering. "There are a good crop of them in the bushes just over there." He pointed into the darkness under the trees. "I am going to gather them."

The tall hermit snorted and stepped in front of Benedict. "And how are you going to carry them with no basket?" He bent down and peered around Benedict. "The outsiders!" He made a grab at Nikki.

Nikki yelped and dodged his grasping arm.

Benedict shoved Nikki and Curio toward the trees. "Run!"

Nikki grabbed Curio by the sleeve of his torn jacket and dashed across the clearing. Behind her she heard a yell and snatched a glance over her shoulder. Benedict had tackled the tall hermit and they were rolling on the ground. Nikki doubled her speed, slowing down only when she felt pine branches scratching at her face.

Curio cried out as he stumbled over a tree root. "Slowly, Miss," he gasped. "It won't do to run in the dark like this. We'll break our necks."

Nikki stopped and turned back toward the clearing, breathing hard. She squinted into the darkness. She could just make out the wrestling forms of Benedict and the other hermit. She turned doubtfully in the other direction, into the forest. "If we go any further into the trees we're going to get hopelessly lost," she said. "Maybe we should wait here for Athena."

Curio gave her a little shove away from the clearing. "Can't, Miss. If we stay here so close to the camp they'll find us for sure. And you'll be thrown into that hut again. No, we must hide."

"But Curio, Athena called this the Trackless Forest. It has no roads or towns. You remember the view from that rock at the imp headquarters, where we had our picnic before the Knights invaded. The forest spread out for miles and miles. It's huge. And we don't even know which direction to head in."

"That's not strictly true, Miss," said Curio, still giving her impatient little shoves further into the trees. "We know that Athena wants us to head for the Southern Castle."

"Yes, I know," said Nikki. "But without Athena we have no hope of finding it."

Curio's breath whistled through his missing front teeth. "We have a bit of hope, Miss. Even in D-ville we've heard of the Southern Castle. It's well known that the Castle lies on the south coast of the Realm. And that the Trackless Forest lies between the Haunted Hills and the south coast. The way I reckon it, when we left the imps' headquarters we went almost straight away from the Haunted Hills, as the crow flies. Which means, to hit the south coast all we have to do is keep going in the same direction. Once we hit the coast we'll be able to follow it south to the king's castle."

Nikki stopped dead in her tracks. "Are you saying we shouldn't wait for Athena?" A horrible feeling of dread shivered up her spine. Athena and Fuzz were her lifeline in the Realm of Reason. She had met them in her world, back at her high school. They were the only link between home and the Realm. She couldn't imagine travelling through the Realm without them. Just thinking about it made her feel like a tiny boat adrift in a vast, unfamiliar ocean. They had already been separated from Fuzz, and from Gwen. She didn't think she could bear to be separated from Athena too. She was about to turn back toward the hermit camp when the sound of a dog barking reached her ears.

"Caliban!" whispered Curio. "Quick, run! Else that hound will sniff out our trail!"

He darted forward into the trees. Nikki let out a cry of frustration. She made a grab for his jacket but he was already out of reach. She had no choice but to follow him. She couldn't leave him all alone in the Trackless Forest.

Nikki found it impossible to catch up to Curio. He seemed to have eyes that could see in the dark. She kept tripping over tangled roots and fallen branches while Curio ran on just out of her reach. After they had run for what seemed like miles the moon suddenly rose above the horizon, shining down through the trees. The light turned the tangled tree roots into masses of writhing snake-shadows, but at least now Nikki could see where she was putting her feet. She caught up to Curio just as he skidded to a halt on the bank of a rushing stream.

"Must go back," Nikki panted, her hands on her knees as she tried to catch her breath. "Get Athena."

Curio ignored her and waded into the water, his arms straight out for balance as the current pushed against his scrawny legs. "This will fool that Caliban," he said. "His nose won't be able to track us in the water."

Instead of crossing the stream as Nikki had expected Curio stayed in the water, walking downstream. Nikki swore under her breath, mentally apologizing to her mother, who didn't like swearing. But this was a swearing moment if ever there was one. She felt torn in two. One half of her wanted to go back to Athena, the other half knew that it couldn't abandon Curio in the Trackless Forest. She gave a loud cry of frustration and followed Curio. Her teeth chattered as she waded along in the icy water, her feet slipping on the moss-covered rocks lining the bottom of the stream. She envied Cation, who was tucked up warm and dry inside the rucksack.

After wading along the stream for a hundred yards or so Curio finally climbed out onto the bank and shook his soaking trousers. "Brr! Cold that was, Miss. But useful. I daresay we don't need to worry about them hermits tracking us anymore."

Nikki shivered violently, tucking her hands into the sleeves of the woolen tunic Fuzz had "borrowed" for her back in Deceptionville. "My guess is that they won't try very hard to find us," she said. "They'll just be glad to be rid of us. You heard what Benedict said. That healer, Brother Jerome, was stirring up the other hermits against us outsiders. It doesn't make any sense that they'd try to bring us back. I'm sure they've given up already and are back at their camp."

"Maybe, Miss," said Curio, "but maybe not. That tall one, the Rounder type, he seemed bent on hurting someone. I know that type well. My master back in Deceptionville was like that. Bullies, they both are. Like to cause pain. He had you down as a target, mark my words. I'd bet a pile of good gold coin that he's angry as a hornet's nest that you escaped. I had to get you away from that camp."

Nikki found it hard to believe she'd ever been in any real danger. The hermits were Athena's friends, after all. But now she had a new worry. "I hope he doesn't try to take his anger out on Athena." She looked back the way they had come. "Maybe we should go back for her."

Curio shook his head as he rang water out of his trouser leg. "She'll be fine, Miss. When I woke from my nap in the tent I nosed around the camp a bit. Heard them having some big meeting in one of the largest cabins. Listened at the window, I did. They were arguing about what to do with you. That bloke called Brother Jerome was wanting to perform some kind of rituals on you. Exorcism, he called it. Don't know what that is, but I didn't like the sound of it at all. Most of them seemed in favor of it, but Athena and that old hermit Prospero were absolutely forbidding it. The meeting got loud, lots of shouting, but at the end Athena and Prospero won out. Old Prospero seems to be some kind of unofficial head of them hermits. They mostly seem to do what he tells them, even if they don't always like it."

Curio rubbed his shivering arms. "As for Athena, Miss. All of them hermits except maybe that Brother Jerome, all of them treated her most politely. Seems to be a favorite among them. Known her for a long time, apparently. She's not in any danger from them. They seem to consider her one of their own. But you, Miss, are another matter. After the meeting I heard that nasty hermit, the tall one, talking with Brother Jerome. Going to go ahead with that exorcism on you, they were. On the quiet. So Prospero and Athena wouldn't know until it was too late."

He shook his head. "Going on and on about demons, they were." He snorted. "Nutty buggers. We got lots of them demon-believers back in D-ville. Crazy as drunken goats, they are. Dangerous, too. They get obsessed. Had a woman killed, we did, last year. One of her neighbors accused her of being possessed by a demon, and to drive it out a bunch of crazies dragged her down to the river and held her under the water until she drowned. You don't want to mess with demon-believers, Miss. That's why, when I heard what Brother Jerome was planning, I ran and found Benedict. Seemed like the best of a nutty bunch, he did. And I was right. He lost no time in letting you out of that hut."

He pointed at Nikki's rucksack. "He also tucked some food in there. Come in handy, it will, as it'll be a long walk to the coast. About three days would be my guess, as long as we don't start walking in circles."

Nikki slid the rucksack off her shoulders and set it on the ground. She opened the top flap and peered inside. A small round of cheese, a bag of dried fruit – cherries by the smell – and one kitten. Cation popped her head out and mewed loudly.

"I bet you're hungry," she said, pulling Cation out of the rucksack. "So am I. Let's have a rest."

Curio nodded eagerly and they sat down with their backs against a tall pine. The ground below the tree was a foot deep in dry pine needles. They burrowed into the needles, heaping them on top of their legs for warmth. Cation curled up in Nikki's lap, eyeing the round of cheese Nikki was examining.

"Curio, do you have a knife?"

"No, Miss. Sorry."

"That's okay. We'll make do." The round of cheese was covered in wax. Beeswax, Nikki guessed. She scraped at it with her fingernails.

"Here, Miss. Try this." Curio held up a small rock with jagged edges.

Nikki attacked the cheese, gouging out bits of wax. "Boy, those hermits really like to protect their cheeses. This stuff is worse than the plastic packaging at the supermarket."

"What's plastic, Miss?"

"It's . . ." Nikki paused, remembering the debate she'd had with herself about introducing new knowledge into the Realm. "It's just a type of wrapping," she finally said. "Like parchment."

She handed Curio a small wedge of cheese she'd managed to excavate from the wax, and then dropped one in her lap in front of Cation.

Cation sniffed suspiciously at her piece of cheese, her ears flat, her whiskers drooping. It was plain she had hoped her snack would be of the chicken variety. A selection from the dairy group was a big disappointment. But she condescended to nibble her way through the chunk anyway, a grouchy look on her face.

As they ate the sun rose. A red glow lit the tops of the trees and crept slowly down to the needle-covered ground, illuminating the purple flowers of a nearby rhododendron bush. Somewhere above them a blue jay cawed. A squirrel scampered down from the tree they were leaning against and sat watching them, its tail twitching eagerly.

Nikki threw the squirrel a dried cherry. It snatched up the wrinkled bit of fruit, stuffed it in its mouth pouch, and edged closer.

Nikki waved at it dismissively. "Sorry. One is all you get."

The squirrel gave her a dirty look and dashed back up the pine tree.

Curio finished his cheese and piled more dry pine needles on top of himself. "We should get some sleep, Miss," he said.

"Now?" asked Nikki. "In the daytime?"

"Yes, Miss. I don't have Miss Athena's forest skills. A city boy I am. Know my way around D-ville's back alleys, but forests are not places I've spent much time in. The only way I can think of to get us to the south coast is to follow the bunny."

Nikki blinked in confusion, looking around the quiet forest for a rabbit scampering under the pines. "What bunny? You mean like rabbit tracks or something?"

Curio shook his head. "No, Miss. The bunny is a constellation in the southern sky. Looks like a rabbit with two big floppy ears. All the kids in D-ville know it, cause of the Day of the Rabbit. It's a big festival held every year, with pastries and candies shaped like rabbits. The festival is held on the day after the bunny first appears in the sky, at the start of spring. It shows up right after dark, and you can see it most of the night. Fortunately it's the start of springtime right now. If we travel by night and aim for the bunny I think we'll eventually reach the south coast. Kind of like Miss Athena was doing when she led us to the hermit camp. But this should be much easier. She had to find a tiny camp in the middle of the Trackless Forest, but we only have to hit the seacoast. Anywhere along it will do. As long as we can keep a straight line we should hit it."

Nikki felt a shiver run up her spine at those words. As long as they could keep a straight line. She'd heard all kinds of stories back home in Wisconsin about people getting lost in the woods. They'd walk in circles until they wore themselves out. It was nearly impossible to keep to a straight line in the woods, not without landmarks, or a road or a river to follow.

A river. "The stream," said Nikki.

"Miss?"

"We need to follow the stream," she said, pointing at the swirling water as it rushed over moss-covered boulders. "Streams join rivers and rivers flow into the sea."

Curio looked doubtful. "I don't know, Miss. Sometimes streams run kind of sideways-like, if hills cut across their path. We'd be better off following the bunny at night."

"We can do both," said Nikki. "We'll try to get some sleep now, and when it's dark we'll head in the direction of the bunny while following the stream at the same time."

"But what if they go in two different directions, Miss?"

"We'll deal with that problem when we come to it," said Nikki with more confidence than she felt. She curled herself up into a ball under the pine needles. Cation tucked herself under Nikki's chin, purring loudly.

It took a long time for Nikki to fall asleep. She lay awake listening to Curio's soft breathing as it whistled through his missing front teeth. Worries chased themselves across her mind. She was worried about Athena, worried about Fuzz and Gwen, worried about getting herself and Curio lost in the Trackless Forest, and worried about whether her Mom was okay back home in Wisconsin. Too many worries. Finally she told herself to just stop thinking. She concentrated on the soothing sound of Cation's purr and eventually fell into a restless sleep.

Chapter Four

—◆●◆—

Sailing Away

NIKKI STAGGERED UP the side of the sand dune and collapsed in a heap at the top. They had done it. They had reached the coast. A salty tang was in the air and below her she could hear waves crashing on the beach, but she was too tired to lift her head to look. Four days it had taken them. Four days of struggling through the tangled undergrowth of the Trackless Forest. Their food had run out on day three. She had given most of it to Curio, pretending to eat pieces of cheese and then tucking them back inside her rucksack.

Now the only thing in her stomach was water from the stream they'd been following. Nikki felt her insides rumble and hoped desperately that the rumbles were just from hunger. She knew from hiking in the Wisconsin woods with her Mom that you could get very sick from drinking out of streams. Bacteria from animal poop got into the water and contaminated it. Neither she nor Curio had been throwing up, though, so maybe they were okay. At least as far as stomach bugs went. Whether they were going to die from starvation was another matter. The rucksack on her back moved and she felt Cation struggle out of it. The kitten mewed loudly.

"I know you're hungry," Nikki muttered, her eyes closed, her face pressed against the sand. "We all are. There's the ocean, right there. Go catch yourself a fish. Catch me one while you're at it."

Cation kneaded Nikki's back with her sharp little claws and mewed even louder.

Nikki ignored her as long as she could. It felt so good just to lie there, resting her aching body and especially her aching feet. The sole of one of her sneakers had caught on a tree root and she had a hole in the bottom of her shoe. Pebbles kept getting in and torturing her foot. If she ever saw Fuzz again she'd have to ask him to "borrow" a pair of boots for her.

Cation gave her a particularly sharp jab with a claw. Nikki groaned and struggled slowly to her feet, lifting Cation off her back before the kitten could dig her claws in even deeper. She peered over the edge of the sand dune. Before her stretched a limitless horizon of ocean. Waves crashed onto the sand and drew back with a pebbly roar. A few dark spots bobbed on the waves, making barking sounds. Seals, she guessed. Nikki knew they were lucky to have reached the coast at all, but she couldn't help feeling discouraged as she looked up and down the empty beach. Sand dunes, sea grass, and seagulls. That was it. No boats, no piers, no fishing villages, nothing. She wondered how far it was to the nearest town. Or even which way it was to the Southern Castle. Should they go up the coast or down?

"Curio!" she called. "Where are you?" There was no sign of him, but as she slid down the sand dune toward the water she noticed a fresh set of tiny footprints in the sand. They marched along the wet sand near the water's edge, aiming for a rocky headland about a quarter mile down the beach.

Nikki headed in the same direction, trudging through the loose dry sand near the dunes. She soon gave this up as too much work. It was like struggling through molasses. She headed for the wet sand just as Curio had done, where the walking was easier. She set Cation down on the sand, out of reach of the waves.

Cation sniffed at a clump of seaweed and stalked for a few paces, picking up her tiny feet and shaking them with each step, as if the wet sand was drenching her delicate fur. She stopped and looked up at Nikki with her ears laid back, a yowl growing in her throat.

"You're becoming a spoiled little princess, you know that?" said Nikki, picking Cation up again.

Cation purred loudly, tucking herself in the crook of Nikki's arm and licking it with her scratchy little tongue.

Nikki set off down the beach again, wondering why Curio had wandered off. It wasn't like him. Since meeting him in Deceptionville he'd attached himself to their little group as if he was a long-lost relative. He'd helped them get Gwen out of the Deceptionville jail and he'd gotten Nikki away from the hermits and their wacky exorcisms. To disappear now seemed strange, but suddenly her nose gave her a clue as to where he'd gone.

Fish. There was a strong smell of fish on the air, and it was not a nasty raw fish smell. It was a wonderful cooked-fish smell. Someone had food and a fire.

Nikki launched into a wobbly jog, her hunger-weakened legs trembling beneath her. Cation yowled and dug in her claws.

"Quiet," said Nikki. "There's food up ahead, you silly little beast. Can't you smell it?"

The rocky headland came nearer and nearer. It was several hundred feet high, with wind-twisted pine trees crowning its summit. To Nikki's dismay she could now see that it reached far into the ocean. Waves were crashing against it, sending clouds of spray into the air. There was no way to walk around it. She'd get dashed against the rocks at its base if she tried. The beach seemed to end at it, as did the line of footprints she was following.

She came to a halt and looked up. There was no way Curio could have climbed the headland. It rose vertically in a daunting, craggy mass of stone. The wind rustled in the pines at its top and tiny Puffin-like birds nested on its side. They launched themselves off the headland like cliff-divers, making little swoops in the air before returning to their nests.

"Curio!" Nikki shouted, her voice drowned out by the crashing waves at the base of the headland.

There was no answer. Nikki reached over her shoulder and tucked Cation into the rucksack. If she had to climb this thing she was going to need her hands free. She walked along the cliff, trying to spot handholds. She couldn't believe Curio had climbed this. It was straight up, even leaning out in several places. Even an experienced rock-climber with ropes and carabiners and stuff would have trouble getting to the top.

Huge boulders clustered at the base of the cliff, covered with lichen and bird poop. Little tide pools full of starfish and spiny purple sea urchins hid in the shadows. Nikki explored behind each boulder, wondering if there was a cave cut into the headland that Curio might be hiding in. She found a few shallow gullies carved into the cliff by wind and water, but no caves.

"Where the heck *are* you, Curio?" she muttered, brushing dirt out of her eyes as she squirmed through a narrow gully, her rucksack scraping its sides. Clumps of dirt showered down on her head and she glanced up worriedly, hoping the cliff wasn't going to slide down on top of her.

Tiny green lizards scooted straight up the cliff-face as she passed. She remembered reading somewhere that certain kinds of lizards could climb straight up because they had millions of tiny hairs on the bottom of their feet which gripped the vertical surface. Usually it was friction and gravity which kept you on a surface. If a person walked up a steep hill it was gravity plus the friction between the soles of their shoes and the ground which kept them from falling. But with lizards and their vertical climbing it wasn't friction but something called directional adhesion. This caused a stickiness so the lizard didn't need to push with a force perpendicular to a vertical surface, such as the side of a cliff. The force needed to push against the cliff would have been much too hard. The lizard would have worn itself out very quickly if each of its feet had to push that hard on each step. Instead the millions of tiny hairs on its feet kept it clinging to the vertical surface.

Nikki stopped, watching the lizards scramble up to the pine trees waving far above her. Curio was a very resourceful kid, but she was pretty sure even he couldn't turn himself into a lizard. No, he must have gotten through this headland somehow, rather than climbing over it.

The gully she was in kept going and going, curving like a winding river and sometimes almost bending back on itself. The sand on the bottom was wet, with small tide pools which she had to jump over. Tiny silver fish, not more than an inch long, swam in the larger pools. The ocean obviously filled this gully at high tide. Nikki hoped the tide wasn't coming in. If the gully came to a dead end and the ocean rushed in, well it wasn't something she wanted to think about.

After a few more windings she noticed that the gully was becoming wider. She could now stretch out her arms to either side, her fingertips barely reaching the sandy walls. The smell of roasting fish was getting stronger and stronger. Suddenly bright sunlight hit her eyes. She stepped out of the gully onto a broad sandy beach. She had come all the way through the rocky headland.

She had expected to find Curio and a campfire. What she saw was Curio, a campfire, a group of strangers, and a huge sailing ship anchored just off the beach.

"Miss!" Curio waved and ran toward her. "Miss, I was just coming to get you." He grabbed her arm and pulled her toward the group around the fire. "They have wonderful grilled codfish, Miss. And a drink called rum which you need to be careful about. It goes down very rough, it does." He brushed the sand off a large piece of driftwood which was pulled up near the fire. "Sit, Miss. I'll make sure you get a nice big fish."

Nikki sat down on the driftwood and eased the rucksack off her back. The strangers numbered about twenty, an intimidating number of people to have staring at you. The staring didn't seem hostile, just curious. Nikki cleared her throat nervously and tried to look friendly.

A woman dressed in a long leather coat and puffy black trousers tucked into black leather boots stepped forward. There were streaks of gray in her wild dark hair and her face was deeply suntanned. Her bright blue eyes contrasted sharply with her tan skin. A sword was buckled at her side.

"Welcome," she said, holding out a calloused hand to Nikki. "I'm called Griff. I'm the captain of that ship yonder and the leader of this band of miscreants."

Nikki jumped up and shook hands, realizing too late that if you haven't eaten for two days jumping up quickly was probably not a good idea. She swayed, her knees trembling. As her eyes started to roll back in her head the woman gently pushed her back down onto the log of driftwood.

"Put your head down between your knees, that's it. You'll feel better after you have a belly full of cod."

Nikki felt something pushed into her hand.

"Hard tack, that is," said the woman. "Sailor's bread. Makes for tough chewing, but it'll settle your stomach."

Nikki mumbled thanks and gnawed warily on a corner of the bread. Tough chewing was right. It was more like a big cracker than bread. A big cracker made out of cement. She managed to get some of it inside her. Her stomach was grateful, but her teeth weren't so sure. Nikki chewed slowly and cautiously. The Realm didn't seem like a good place to have dental problems. No Novocain or fillings here. Judging by Curio's permanently missing front teeth the custom was to let damaged teeth fall out or even worse, to pull them out. Nikki shuddered.

"Cold, she is. Poor little thing."

Nikki felt a rough, smelly woolen blanket wrapped around her. "Thanks," she said to the stout little woman who was tucking the blanket around her.

"No problem, dearie," said the woman. "Can't have you freezing to death. This wind's enough to freeze the fins off a codfish." She pulled the hood of her patched wool coat over her white hair and shivered.

Nikki studied her, a bit surprised by her presence in the group. They were obviously the crew of the huge sailing ship anchored off the beach. Griff, the captain, was about her Mom's age, she guessed, but the rest were mostly young men. This white-haired woman, though, looked very old. In her seventies, even eighties. Nikki wondered how such an elderly person could cope with the hardships of a life at sea.

The elderly woman laughed. "You're wondering what an old stump like me is doing sailing the high seas, aren't you dearie? Well, I'll tell you. Born on a ship, I was. Spent my whole life on them. Name's Posie. Short for Poseidon, that is. Him what's the ruler of the oceans. Both me Mam and me Dad were sailors. I've salt water in me veins."

"Posie is our cook," said Griff. "And a mighty fine one she is. Our bellies would be much emptier without her. She can make even seaweed stew tasty." She gave the elderly woman a gentle push toward the fire, where a grill made of driftwood and iron bars had been setup over the coals. "Now, Posie, do your duty and give our guest a nice chunk of grilled cod."

"Coming right up," said Posie, bending over the coals.

"And another for me, Ma'am," piped up Curio, who was sitting cross-legged on the sand close to the fire, warming his hands. "I could eat a whole school of fish, I'm that hungry."

Posie chuckled. "I'll slap another on the grill for you, young man. Can't have childrens a'goin hungry. Still growin', you are, and the young lady also, though she's got a good ten inches of height on you. A little shrimp, you are."

Curio shrugged good-naturedly. "Always been so, Ma'am. Can't complain. Useful, it is, sometimes. Back in D-ville I could slip through the crowds and no one noticed me. It's a good thing to go unnoticed. Specially in D-ville, with all its Rounders and Lurkers and other nasty types. Dead useful being able to slide right through the tightest gaps when you see those types coming."

"So you're from D-ville, are you?" asked Griff, looking from Curio to Nikki. "Long ways from home, you two are."

"I'm D-ville bred and born, Ma'am," said Curio. "Miss Nikki here is not, as you can probably tell by her good manners. Us D-villers aren't known for our good breeding."

The captain looked down at Nikki thoughtfully. "No, now that you mention it, your speech isn't that of D-ville. Spent some time there, in my youth. Glad to leave the place, I was. A person can breathe free on the open seas. In the dirty alleys of D-ville the smells and the dirt choke your lungs."

Nikki smiled up at her politely, hoping she was going to drop the topic of hometowns. She wasn't sure how this band of sailors, who she knew nothing about, would react to the news that she wasn't from the Realm at all. Back in Deceptionville Fuzz had warned her to hide the fact that she was a stranger in the Realm, and it still seemed like a good idea. Some people, like Gwen and Curio, hadn't cared, but her frightening treatment by the hermits in the Trackless Forest had proven that others in the Realm were extremely suspicious of outsiders.

Griff seemed to sense that Nikki was uncomfortable with the topic. She turned and waved a hand across the band of sailors who were lounging on the sand, picking at fishbones. She named them one by one, so quickly that Nikki promptly forgot all of the names she had just heard. Most were strong-looking young men who looked like they could hoist sails in a flash and pull up heavy anchors in a rough sea. Three of the band caught her eye because they were different from the others. One was an imp who reminded her a bit of Fuzz, though Fuzz was younger and had a rascally twinkle in his eye that this imp definitely did not. He glared at Nikki from under bushy gray eyebrows when he caught her staring at him. Nikki quickly looked away.

The other two who stood out from the group were clearly brother and sister. They looked so alike Nikki guessed that they must be fraternal twins. They were younger than the other sailors, maybe in their late teens, and they were the first black inhabitants of the Realm Nikki had seen. The girl had her hair twisted into dreadlocks with shiny blue ribbons braided through it. The boy had a wild puff of hair that surrounded his head like dandelion fuzz. They were both dressed in what looked like deerskin tunics and pants. The girl smiled at her and the boy winked when he saw her staring at them.

Nikki smiled back. It might be nice to talk to someone close to her own age, she thought. Curio, for all his resourcefulness, was still very much a young boy. Nikki felt responsible for him, which led to worrying about him, which was kind of tiring after a while. She wasn't used to it, not having any brothers or sisters back home in Wisconsin. She'd never even taken care of any pets. Her Mom was allergic to both cats and dogs. And now here she was in a strange land, trying to look after a ten-year-old boy and a kitten.

As if she knew Nikki was thinking about her Cation popped her head out of the rucksack. She looked warily around at all the strangers, but the smell of roasting fish finally became too much for her and she hopped down to the sand, mewing loudly.

"Aw, look at the wee little fuzzball," said Posie, holding her hand out for Cation to sniff.

Cation licked avidly at the cook's fishy-smelling fingers.

Posie laughed and pulled a large chunk of half-cooked fish off the grill, laying it in the sand at the kitten's feet.

Cation pounced on it, snatching it up in her mouth and carrying it off to a nearby sand dune to feast on it in peace.

Nikki watched nervously as a seagull which had been hovering nearby made a beeline for the kitten. A hawk could tear Cation apart in seconds, but she wasn't sure about a seagull. It was probably just after the piece of fish, but just in case. . . She was just about to go after the kitten and bring her back to the fire when the gull suddenly dive-bombed Cation. Cation hissed like a cobra and threw herself into the air, taking a vicious swipe at the seagull. Her tiny claws connected with the gull's wing, scattering feathers on the sand. The gull screeched and flew off to safer territory.

Posie guffawed, slapping her knees. "What a little pirate! She'll make a fine addition to the crew. Make short work of the rats on the ship, she will."

"An addition to the crew?" said Nikki. "But, she's mine." She was surprised to find tears in her eyes. She wiped at them impatiently.

Posie shuffled over to her and patted her on the back. "Aw, honey, no one's gonna take your kitty. I just meant that maybe she could have a go at the rats while you three are sailing with us."

"I told them about our needing to get to the Southern Castle, Miss," said Curio. "To meet up with Miss Athena and Mr. Fuzz. Lots easier, it'll be, to sail there instead of walking the whole way."

"Oh," said Nikki, looking at Griff. "That's very nice of you. To take us along, I mean. I hope it's not out of your way."

Griff shrugged good-naturedly. "We were headed in that direction anyway. And it's a good place to pick up supplies."

"From the castle?" asked Nikki in surprise.

Griff laughed. "That's rich. No, somehow I don't think that old goat Maleficious would be too generous with his barrels of pork and rum. No, there's a large town below the castle. A trading port called Kingston. A bit rough around the edges, as ports always are, but mostly it's a decent place. We always put in there when sailing the south coast."

"Maleficious is at the Southern Castle?" asked Nikki worriedly. Her encounter with the king's advisor at Castle Cogent hadn't gone well. She'd prefer never to meet him again. And the things Athena had told her about him, his hatred of the imps, hadn't improved her opinion of him.

"He's rarely there in person," said Griff. "He spends most of his time at Castle Cogent, which is the main seat of power in the Realm. If there's anything old Maleficious loves it's power. But he has minions all over the Realm. A little snot by the name of Rufius is his favorite. Rufius is seen at the Southern Castle from time to time, lording it over the local population and manipulating the King when he's in residence."

"Great," said Nikki, sighing. Rufius again. He was tied with Maleficious, Avaricious and Fortuna as her least favorite person in the Realm.

Griff grinned at her. "I can see you've had dealings with the little piece of dirt."

Nikki nodded. "I was travelling with two imps called Fuzz and Athena. They're the King's emissaries, as Athena loves to point out at every opportunity. We were on the Isle of Ignorance when we first met Rufius. He was hanging around a stall which sold weird, superstitious stuff like evil eyes and charms written on scraps of parchment. Athena thought he was wonderful, at first. She's very fond of cleanliness. You should see her gray woolen dress. It's absolutely spotless, even after she's been on the road for weeks. I don't know how she does it. Anyway, Rufius is like that too. There's never a speck of dirt on his tunics or his sandals. I thought it was creepy, but Athena thought it was proof of his good character. Boy, was she wrong. We saw Rufius again at the tent of a fortune teller called Fortuna, and then again at the estate of a knight called Sir Cadwan. We started to think that he was following us. Fuzz was suspicious of him from the start. But Athena ignored Fuzz's warnings until we met Rufius again at Muddled Manor, a large estate not far from the Haunted Hills. It was at Muddled Manor that we found out who Rufius really was. We were having tea with Lady Ursula, owner of the Manor, when Rufius revealed that he worked for Maleficious. Athena and Fuzz left the Manor immediately."

The imp in the group suddenly spoke in his gravelly voice. "Aye, no imp would stay after hearing that," he said. "Not after the forced evacuations of imps from so many towns in the Realm. All Maleficious's doing." He spat on the sand.

Griff nodded sadly. "Tis a shame. Relations in the Realm between imps and us big people used to be friendly. Everyone lived side-by-side and traded in the marketplace with no problems. Imps like your Fuzz and Athena held high positions at the king's court, and in town halls and councils throughout the land. You don't see that much anymore. They've been pressured to resign. Their families get threatened if they don't. No imp's been killed yet, at least not that I've heard, but it's just a matter of time. The rumors are the worst. Maleficious deliberately spreads rumors which blame the imps for any bad thing which happens in the Realm. It's turned people against them."

"Pigs," said the gravel-voiced imp. "Used to live on a pig farm, I did. Near the Isle of Ignorance. Two years ago a disease started killing off the pigs. The landowner called in animal doctors, all kinds of farming experts, but nobody could stop it. Half the pigs died. And no one would touch the meat. The landowner had to sell the farm and move to a broken-down house on the edge of town. Rumors started flying that I'd cursed the pigs. Used some kind of fancy imp-magic." He snorted. "If I'd had magic I'd have cursed the rumor-spreading idiots, not the pigs." He snapped a fishbone in two. "Spent the next year scratching out a living on the Isle of Ignorance, working at a stall in the market selling beets. Good way to starve. No profit in beets.

Finally I headed for the coast to try my hand at fishing. Worked on a few boats and got pretty good at spotting schools of cod. Learned their ways, where they spawn, what islands they like to gather near, what currents they ride."

"Tarn's the best spotter on the south coast," said Griff. "That's what we do. Sail the coast looking for schools of fish. Cod, mostly, but also mackerel, tuna, salmon. Sell our information to the highest bidders at the fishing ports." She grinned. "We used to do a little fishing ourselves, but that's hard work, that is. Selling information is a much easier way to make a living than hauling on nets all day."

"Okay, enough chit-chat," broke in Posie. "The young lass is hungry for food, not words." She handed Nikki a chunk of grilled fish, filleted on a piece of driftwood. "You just gobble that right down, dearie. There's more when you're ready."

After three helpings of grilled fish and a jug full of spring water Nikki felt more like herself. She tried a sip of rum, but it felt like she was swallowing hot tar. After coughing so hard she thought she was going to cough up a lung she refused to drink anymore, which caused a few laughs among the crew. Curio swallowed quite a bit of the stuff. He seemed to have a taste for it, which Nikki found worrisome. He was slurring his words, giggling to himself as he produced a high-pitched whistle from between his missing front teeth, and wobbling around the fire on his scrawny little legs. Nikki made a mental note to keep him away from the rum bottle from now on. She felt like Athena, always trying to keep Fuzz away from taverns. Hopefully she'd have more success with Curio than Athena had with Fuzz.

Griff clapped her hands. "Right, troops. You've had a nice rest, been fed and watered. Time to get back to the ship."

Griff and Posie dismantled the grill and stamped out the fire.

Nikki rounded up Curio and Cation. She tucked the well-fed and purring kitten back into her rucksack.

The rest of the crew grabbed barrels from a pile not far away and hoisted them onto their shoulders.

"Water," said Tarn, who was not carrying a barrel. "Nice spring nearby. Even sailors need a break from rum sometimes." He shot a glance at Nikki and laughed rather meanly.

"Don't mind him," said the girl with the ribbons in her hair, who was also not carrying a barrel. "Tarn's more bark than bite. Aren't you, you wee leetle imp?" She ruffled Tarn's hair.

The imp jumped away from her, muttering curses.

The girl laughed. "Don't worry, he's harmless. Still, it might be better to give him a wide berth. Has a bitter streak, Tarn does. No denying it. Can't really blame him, after the way he was treated back in his hometown. And he doesn't take well to strangers. Me and Krill were on board for more than a year before he finally spoke to us."

"Is Krill your brother?" asked Nikki as they walked along the beach toward the anchored ship.

"Aye, twins we are," said the girl. "I'm Kira. We're from Suria. That's a land far from here, not part of the Realm. Across the ocean, it is. Very hot and full of palm trees and flowers. Lots of bugs, too. Don't remember much about it. Me and Krill were taken by pirates when we were wee little buggers. Grabbed right out of our beds."

"That's terrible," said Nikki. "I'm so sorry."

Kira shrugged. "Don't really remember it. I was only five or six. Hazy, it is, in my mind. Krill remembers more. He says I've blocked it out. Anyway, the pirates took us all the way to Kingston and sold us to a rich merchant who used us as household slaves. We cleaned floors, turned the spit for the roasts, peeled potatoes, carried in water and carried out chamber pots. We were locked in at night so we couldn't escape. Wouldn't have known where to go, anyway. Can't exactly own a home or start up a business when you're only six years old. It was Griff who saved us from that life. We'd been slaves for four years when one day Krill and me was sent down to the docks to buy fish for that night's dinner. Griff was sitting on a barrel mending a net. She gave us a friendly 'hello', which took us by surprise, I can tell you. People in the Realm are mostly nice enough folks, but they aren't used to seeing people who look like Krill and me. They avoid us, to put it plainly. But not Griff. She was sweet as honey to us, right from the start. Asked us where our parents were, and when we told her about cleaning the floors and carrying the chamber pots she asked us if we wanted to join her crew. We've been sailing with her ever since. It's not a bad life. Krill likes the physical stuff, hauling on ropes, raising the sails. Me, I'm the navigator. Griff taught me, after she discovered that I had a knack for it."

"What does a navigator do?" asked Nikki, scratching Cation under the chin. The kitten had poked her head out of the rucksack and was batting at Nikki's ear with a sheathed paw.

"I tell the crew where to steer the ship," said Kira. "Griff makes the final decision, of course, but mostly it's up to me to keep us on course."

"How do you know where to go?" asked Nikki.

"I use a sextant," said Kira.

Nikki nodded. "We have those in my wor . . .I mean, I've heard of those. Though I don't know how to use one." Tired of getting a paw poked in her ear, she shoved a complaining Cation back down into the depths of the rucksack. The rucksack growled all the way to the ship.

"I'll show you, if you want" said Kira. "It's not hard. When we're sailing along a coast like we are today I don't need it. We just follow the coastline. But when we're searching for schools of fish we often head out into deep waters, far from land. It's then that I use the sextant. By day I use it to measure the angle of the sun relative to the horizon, and by night I measure the angle of certain stars, either relative to the horizon or relative to the moon."

"Um, okay," said Nikki uncertainly.

"It's easier than it sounds," said Kira. "I'll show you tonight. As long as you're not spilling your guts all over the deck. How are your sea legs?"

"I don't get seasick, if that's what you mean," said Nikki. "My Mom and I went on a two-week sailing course on Lake Michigan last year. That's a really big lake in my, um, Realm. It's bigger than some seas, and has huge waves just like an ocean. I didn't get sick once."

"That's good," said Kira. "Some people get so sick on a ship that they're totally useless. They just lie on the deck and groan."

Nikki set her shoulders, determined not to be totally useless. They were close to the ship now. It was anchored about thirty yards from shore and loomed above the beach like a floating fortress. It looked much more intimidating close up than it had from back by the fire. The ship rocked slightly as gentle waves rolled under it. Its sails were furled. A complicated-looking web of ropes, masts and pulleys rose above the wooden hull. The tallest mast was higher than a three-story building. At the bow a carved wooden codfish served as figurehead.

The crew loaded their barrels of water onto two dinghies which had been pulled up onto the sand. Nikki followed Kira over to one of them and they climbed in, hauling Curio up after them. The three of them took a seat in the bow, out of the way of the sailors. After all the water barrels were loaded the sailors shoved the boat into the water and waded into the waves, pulling themselves up over the side. Two sailors grabbed the oars and stroked toward the ship.

As they approached the ship Nikki noticed a rope ladder dangling over the side. She glanced at Curio worriedly. He was still mumbling to himself and rocking back and forth. "Curio, are you going to be okay climbing that?" she asked, pointing at the rope ladder.

Curio squinted at it, his mouth slack. "Sure, Miss. Of course. Wondersful at climbering stuff, I is. Don't you worries."

Kira giggled. "Your little companion can't hold his rum. Shouldn't be drinking so much of it at his age. Griff's a great captain, but she sometimes forgets that kids are kids. She had me and Krill drinking rum soon as we joined her crew. Fortunate it was that neither of us had a taste for it. Sometimes we're the only two in the whole crew who aren't drunk out of our minds. Though they mostly save the heavy drinking for when we're in port, which is a good thing, as manning a ship this big with only two is nigh near impossible."

The dinghy bumped against the hull of the ship, rocking slightly on the waves. Kira grabbed the end of the rope ladder and climbed up it quick as a cat.

Nikki grabbed the end of the ladder and tried to hold it steady. "Okay, Curio. Up you get. Take your time." She hauled Curio up with her free hand and kept a hand on his back while he balanced unsteadily on the bow of the dinghy.

"No problems, Miss. This easys as pies," he slurred, and promptly fell overboard with a splash.

The sailors on the dinghy roared with laughter. One of them reached a sinewy arm over the side and plucked Curio out of the water as easily as snatching a drowned rat by the tail. The sailor, still laughing, tucked Curio under one arm and climbed up the rope ladder one-handed.

Nikki followed, not quite as nimbly. The rope ladder flapped against the hull of the ship with each wave, painfully banging her knuckles against the side. She realized that the way to avoid bruised knuckles was to climb as rapidly as possible. She increased her speed, trying to remember all the rope climbs she'd done in PE class. Of course, in PE class the rope hadn't been attached to a swaying ship. When she finally reached the top Kira helped her clamber over the wooden railing which ran along the hull.

The sailor who'd carried Curio up deposited him on a pile of coiled rope. Nikki checked that Curio was okay and then turned in a slow circle, gazing in awe at the huge ship. The main mast towered above her, a crows nest on top swaying back and forth with the waves. Above the crows nest a flag flapped in the breeze, blue with a school of silver fish flashing across it. Squawking seagulls perched on the rigging and a creaking noise came from the hull as its timbers were pushed and pulled by the sea beneath it.

In front of her rose a short flight of steps leading up to a wooden platform. At the top was the ship's tiller, a large wooden wheel with spokes all around it. Below the platform another flight of steps led down below deck into the quarters for the captain and crew.

Nikki jumped as something slithered around her leg. She looked down to find a cat sitting on its haunches, starting up at her. It was the ugliest cat she'd ever seen. Its fur was sewage-brown and large patches of it were missing. The exposed skin was raw and scaly. The cat had only one eye. Where the other one should have been was only a bumpy scar.

"That's just ole Scratch," said Posie, unhooking her arms from around the neck of the sailor who'd given her a lift up the rope ladder. "He's harmless, dearie. Well, maybe he bites now and then, but he don't draw much blood. Not the purtiest thing, I'll admit, but he's a marvel at rat-catching. We used to be knee-deep in the varmints until we got ole Scratch." She playfully rubbed the cat's head and the cat not so playfully bit her finger. Posie just laughed and headed below deck, leaving Nikki and the cat staring at each other.

"Um, hello," said Nikki.

Scratch just stared at her, or rather stared at Nikki's rucksack as Cation's head popped out of it. Scratch's eye gleamed red. His haunches bunched, ready to jump.

Nikki backed away from him, wagging a finger. "Oh no you don't. You leave Cation alone. Go back to your rat-catching."

Cation climbed onto Nikki's shoulder to get a better look at Scratch. Apparently she didn't like what she saw, for her ears laid back and she hissed as fiercely as when the seagull had dive-bombed her.

Scratch crouched down, assuming attack position again.

"Not so fast, you mangy fiend," said Griff, scooping up Scratch and tossing him onto a nearby barrel. "Keep a close eye on your kitten while you're on board. Scratch's been known to eat other cats. If he wasn't such a good ratter I'd have got rid of him long ago." She went over to Curio, who had curled up on the pile of rope and was sound asleep. She motioned to a sailor, who slung Curio over his shoulder and carried him below deck.

"We'll let him sleep it off," said Griff. "Wake up with a headache, he will, but otherwise he'll be fine. Come up to the quarterdeck. We're just about ready to cast off."

The casting off process turned out to be quite complicated, with Griff shouting orders and the sailors rushing around pulling up anchors, hauling on ropes and raising the sails. Kira was at the helm, calmly turning the ship's wheel with one-hand as the sails caught the wind and the ship lurched forward.

Nikki watched it all from her perch on top of a barrel which was lashed to the side of the ship with iron chains. She was a bit alarmed at first when the ship seemed to be headed straight out to sea, but after a while she noticed that they were slowly headed down the coast. The ship zig-zagged back and forth to catch the wind. Tacking, it was called. She tried to remember what she'd learned at sailing camp. From the way the blue fish-flag was pointed she could tell that the wind was coming at the bow of the ship, which meant that to go forward they had to tack from close haul to close haul. Close haul meant the sails were set at a forty-five degree angle away from the wind. To hold course Kira turned the wheel, which was the ship's tiller or steering mechanism, from one close haul position to the opposite one, or from a ten o'clock position to a two o'clock position and then back again. Nikki noticed that Kira was turning the wheel in the opposite direction from where the ship went. If Kira turned the wheel to the right the ship swung left. That meant the ship had an old pulley and rope system which connected the tiller directly to the ship's rudder. The sailboats Nikki's sailing camp had used were a much more modern design, with a gear system below deck which allowed the tiller to act more like the steering wheel of a car. If you turned the tiller left the boat also went left. She supposed Kira was used to it, but Nikki found it confusing. The boat kept going in the opposite direction from what she expected.

"A beauty, isn't she?" said Griff, her arm sweeping the ship from bow to stern. "Sunfish, she's called. The crew wanted to name her Codfish, seeing as that's what we mostly search for, but I stomped on that idea right quick. Codfish is no name for a ship. Kira's got things well in hand. Want to see below decks?"

Nikki nodded vigorously. "Yes, please. Can I see the tiller mechanism?"

Griff's eyebrows raised in surprise. "Certainly, if you wish. It's down in the hold. Not a request I get very often."

"It's kind of a hobby," said Nikki. "I like seeing how things work."

"Well, I'm sorry to say I won't be able to dazzle you," said Griff, leading the way down the stairs and into the depths of the hold. They passed sleeping quarters with bunks and hammocks and continued down past storerooms piled high with boxes and barrels. "She's a good ship, she is, but Sunfish's not state of the art. Her mechanism is simple. Simple enough so that my even my most lunkheaded crew member can repair it in a storm if he needs to."

As they reached the dark hold a strong smell of brine and barnacles wafted up from the floor, which was damp from salt water. Unpleasant little ratty squeaks echoed from the wooden beams overhead.

"Got to lock that demon Scratch down here again," said Griff. "The rat population's multiplying. He's been shirking his duties. Prefers lying in the sun above decks, he does, but that's not what he's on board for."

"Maybe my cat could help," said Nikki. "Though I wouldn't want her locked in down here."

"Nah," said Griff. "Posie was only joking about that. We got rats down here could swallow your little kitten in one gulp. You keep her tucked up safe in that sack of yours while you're on board."

Griff paused, water lapping at her boots. "Have a bit of a leak down here. Not unusual. I'll get Sunfish a fresh coat of tar on her hold when we pull into port in Kingston." She pointed up at a shaft of light which poured through a narrow opening over their heads. "The ship's wheel is right above that opening. See those two round posts? They're called sheaves. There's a rope which goes around the axle of the wheel and then around those two posts."

They walked over to the starboard side of the ship.

Nikki followed Griff's pointing finger as it traced a rope which led from the starboard sheave to a pulley mounted on the hull of the ship and then to a vertical wooden post which went through the floor down into the water.

"That's the rudder stock," said Griff, pointing at the post, which was slowly turning. "It's attached to the rudder, which is in the water directly below us. The rudder is what turns the ship. Just a big wooden paddle, the rudder is. As I said, simple to understand. Simple to repair. People like the King or the rich merchants in Kingston have ships with steering mechanisms that are a lot more complicated. Fancy gears and stuff which makes the ship easier to steer, easier to handle with fewer crew members. But that fancy stuff comes at a price. Needs a specialist on board to fix it if something goes wrong. And something always goes wrong, usually when you're miles from land."

Nikki bent down and peered through the narrow opening between the rudder stock and the hull. She could hear waves crashing against the hull but couldn't see much. She tried to imagine the giant wooden rudder as it turned from side to side, and tried to remember what the coach at her sailing camp had said about steering a sailboat. The water pushing on one side of the rudder created a force which turned the boat. Turbulence was created on the lee side of the rudder, the side opposite the water flow. This turbulence created a drag which slowed the boat down. A well-designed rudder would be shaped to produce as little drag as possible. The boat's keel was also involved in turning the boat. Small sailboats had removable keels called center-boards, which were just a board in the middle of the hull which stuck straight down into the water. A big ship like the Sunfish would have a fixed keel – a large tapered section of the hull which also stuck straight down into the water. The keel kept the wind from blowing the boat sideways, making it easier to keep the boat on course.

"What shape is your rudder?" Nikki asked.

"Shape?" asked Griff. "It's just a big wooden paddle, as I said."

"Yes, I know," said Nikki. "But the shape matters a lot. Different shapes create different amounts of drag."

Griff shrugged. "Don't know what in blazes you're talking about. A rudder's a rudder and that's all there is to it."

Nikki sighed. She wished Gwen was on board. Gwen would have been fascinated by rudder design. And she probably knew a lot about turbulence from her studies of the bridge that collapsed into the Deceptionville river.

"C'mon," said Griff, heading toward the stairs. "Let's get back up on deck. Have to keep an eye on my crew. They slack off when they think no one's watching."

"NO, HOLD IT like this." Kira took the sextant from Nikki and held it up to her own eye. "You look through the eyepiece, like this. Focus on Venus. It's off to our right, just above the horizon. When you can see it clearly in this little square mirror then you read the angle off of the arc."

Nikki and Kira were on the quarterdeck. Each had a rough woolen blanket around her shoulders to ward off the nighttime chill. The winds had died down, settling to a reliable breeze coming from the north, which gently pushed the ship south along the coast. The sails were set to the breeze and most of the crew was lounging about, drinking or throwing dice. Curio, still a little groggy from his first experience with rum, was enveloped in a blanket and perched on a barrel nearby. The imp Tarn was also watching them, occasionally throwing out comments which Kira mostly ignored.

"Saturn makes a better guide, Miss know-it-all," called out Tarn. "Gives a better southern reckoning this time of year."

Kira sighed. "Saturn hasn't risen yet, Tarn. How am I supposed to take its reading if it isn't even in the sky yet? Won't be for hours." She handed the sextant back to Nikki. "Here, try again."

Nikki took the strangely-shaped instrument in both hands. It was heavy and made of brass, with two small mirrors and an eyepiece. Below the mirrors was a semi-circle also made of brass, with little tick marks all along it, marking degrees from zero to one-hundred and twenty.

"Now, point the eyepiece at the horizon," said Kira.

Nikki tried, but it was easier said than done on a rolling ship. She widened her stance and braced her elbows against her sides. Better. She could see the faint spot of light which was the planet Venus reflected in the little square mirror. She lowered the sextant and examined it more closely. The eyepiece didn't allow her to look directly at a planet or star, instead the starlight was bounced off of two little mirrors and then into the eyepiece. If she kept the eyepiece level with the horizon the tick marks along the arc told her the angle the star made with the horizon. And that angle could be used to plot the ship's position at sea.

She bent down so that she could view the sextant in the light from the lantern at her feet. She checked the arc angle. "Venus is about twenty degrees above the horizon."

Kira took the sextant and looked through the eyepiece, aligning the instrument with practiced ease. "Yep, twenty, maybe twenty-two degrees." She handed the sextant back to Nikki and took out a piece of parchment and a stubby lead pencil. "We mark down the altitude of the planet or star, in this case Venus at an altitude of twenty-two degrees, and then we mark down the time." She held up the lantern and squinted at a row of hourglasses which were lined up on a nearby barrel. "The big one is for hours, the middle one for minutes, and the small one for seconds."

"You have to mark the time all the way down to the second?" asked Nikki.

Kira nodded. "Have to. If the time is off by more than five seconds that means your position calculation will be off by a whole nautical mile. Easy to get lost at sea if you're sloppy about your readings. Of course, as I said before, right now we don't need the sextant to find our position. We're just following the coastline south to Kingston. I only get out the sextant when we head out into the open ocean, far from land."

"Gotten us lost more than once, haven't you, Miss Navigator?" said Tarn snarkily.

Kira shrugged. "The sextant is a new instrument. Have to get used to it and its workings, don't I? You couldn't do any better, you wee leetle imp."

"Bet I could," said Tarn. "But it's more fun to watch you get us lost." He spat on the deck. "Get us stranded at sea one more time and Griff'll toss you overboard. See if she doesn't."

Kira ignored him, fiddling with a knob on the sextant which reset the mirror positions.

Nikki frowned, peering at the hourglasses. "How do you know what time it is? I mean, you just turned over the hourglasses when we started taking readings with the sextant. We know how long it's been since we started, but not what time of day it is. You're using them more like stopwatches than like a clock."

"We go by Tarn Time," said Kira with a little smirk. "We have another set of hourglasses down in the crew's cabin, and it's Tarn's job to turn them over every hour. He marks the time when we leave a port and keeps a log of every time he turns over an hourglass. That way we can keep track of the time. It's not a perfect system, but we can generally get a good idea of our position, at least if our timekeeper does his job."

"I'll do my job and you do yours, Miss Bossy," huffed Tarn. He glared at Nikki. "And not convinced, I am, that you should be giving away all our secrets to strangers. She'll likely sell our methods to the fishing fleets and then we'll be out of business. If they can find their own cod they won't need us, will they?"

Kira waved a hand dismissively. "Just knowing our methods is useless without a sextant, and we're the only ship in the Realm which has one."

Nikki's eyebrows raised. "Really? This is the only one in existence?"

"The only one on a working vessel," said Kira. "The Prince has several prototypes, but this is the only one in use by a sailing ship."

"Who's the Prince?" asked Nikki.

It was Kira's turn to be astonished. "Who is the Prince! You really are a stranger around here, aren't you? I thought everyone in the Realm had heard of the Prince. His real name is Prince Valdemar, but everyone calls him the Prince of Physics. He's a cousin of the King, and lives in a big fancy mansion in Kingston, not far from the King's castle." She carefully buffed the little square mirrors on the sextant with a bit of cloth. "He invented the sextant. Made this one with his own hands."

Nikki was vividly reminded of Gwen's "invention" of steel, and how disappointed Gwen had been to learn that steel had been discovered centuries ago in Nikki's world. She wasn't sure how long ago sextants had been invented in her own world, but she knew they'd been around for hundreds of years. Though she wasn't going to tell Kira that. She noticed that Kira was suddenly peering at her closely.

"Back on the beach you mentioned that you'd heard of sextants," said Kira, frowning. "I don't see how that's possible, if you've never heard of the Prince. Sextants didn't exist until a year ago, when the Prince showed this one to Griff when we were docked in Kingston. Griff's an old friend of his. I think her family's distantly related to his or something."

Tarn stopped his angry muttering and was also watching her closely.

"Um," stalled Nikki, thinking quickly. "I must have been thinking of something else. Some other instrument. Because now that I see what a sextant looks like, well, I was wrong. I've never seen one before."

Kira and Tarn both continued to stare at her. Kira curiously and Tarn suspiciously.

Nikki cleared her throat. "So, the Prince made this, huh? He must be a remarkable person."

"He is," said Kira, lovingly tucking the sextant back into its leather case. "He's the most famous inventor in the Realm, maybe in all the realms. You might be lucky enough to meet him. He frequently invites Griff to his home when we're in Kingston, and sometimes I get to come along. He likes me because I can sometimes understand him when he's explaining his latest invention. I don't understand everything, of course. The Prince has studied for years and years. He knows all about mathematics, alchemy, metalworking, and a new branch of knowledge which he calls Physics. No one except him really knows what he means by it, but he told me this sextant uses Physics in its workings."

Nikki hoped that she'd get a chance to introduce Gwen to this Prince. He sounded like her twin. They'd be off together experimenting and calculating two seconds after meeting. Behind her she heard Curio give a big yawn. "This has been really interesting," she said to Kira. "Thanks for showing me the sextant, but I think Curio should get to bed. I'm a little tired myself, I have to admit. We had a rough journey before we met up with you."

Curio nodded groggily, nearly falling off his barrel.

"Of course," said Kira. "Follow me. Our quarters are pretty cramped, but we'll make room for you. You two can bunk with Krill and me. If Krill snores just throw something at him."

Chapter Five

❦

Kingston

"**S**MELLS LIKE FISH," said Curio, wrinkling his nose.

Kira laughed. "Of course it smells like fish, wee little man. It's a port. All ports smell like fish. Did you expect it to smell like honeysuckle and roses?"

Nikki, Curio and Kira were leaning over the side of the Sunfish, watching as the crew unloaded empty barrels to be filled with supplies from Kington's market. Cation was perched on Nikki's shoulder, one eye on the piles of freshly-caught fish heaped on the dock, and one eye on Scratch. Scratch was winding himself around Nikki's legs, leering up at Cation. Every so often Nikki would give her leg a shake, trying to convince Scratch to go elsewhere, but it was no use. He stuck to her like a burr, making an ugly, oily sound which might have been purring. Cation's hisses only increased his attempts to fake a purr.

"Can't tell if the old devil wants to eat her or court her," said Posie, scooping up a squirming Scratch. "Glad to see your kitty's still in one piece, no thanks to old Scratch here." She laughed as Scratch wriggled out of her arms and dashed down the ship's gangplank. "He's off to cause his usual mischief. Has lady cats he visits all over town. If Kingston is overflowing with ugly kittens you can bet old Scratch is the cause. You three going into town?"

"Yes, ma'am," said Kira. "Thought I'd show 'em around. See the sights."

Posie frowned. "Best take Krill with you," she said. "Kingston's no place for three little 'uns like yourselves. Not nowadays."

Kira bristled, drawing herself up to her not very impressive height. She was a few years older than Nikki, but not much taller. "I can look after them just fine," she said. "Been roaming around Kingston since I was six years old."

"Roaming around with your brother, you mean," said Griff, coming up the gangplank. "You listen to Posie. She's older and wiser than you."

"Well, she's older anyway," muttered Kira under her breath. "Come on, you two. Let's get off this ship. Krill's down there by the mackerel nets."

"We're meeting at Gray's Inn, round about six in the evening," Griff called after them as they headed down the gangplank. "Make sure you're at the inn by then. Don't want you out by yourselves after dark."

Kira waved a hand in salute and leaped gracefully into the air like a trapeze artist, swinging from one of the ropes which anchored the Sunfish to the dock. She flew through the air and landed light as a feather on the fish-scaled timbers of the dock.

Nikki and Curio followed less acrobatically, stepping carefully down the steep gangplank.

"You've been assigned babysitting duty," announced Kira to her brother, who was deep in conversation with a group of sailors mending the mackerel nets. "Griff's orders."

Krill turned and surveyed the three of them, towering over them with his hands on his hips, his puff of hair blowing in the breeze off the ocean. "I don't think so, sis," he drawled. "Got some grown-up business to attend to. You three run along and play."

Kira snorted. "Grown-up business my fanny. You're just getting your bet in for this evening's dice game. You'll lose like you always do, brother me dear."

Krill grinned good-naturedly. "Win. Lose. It's all part of the fun. And why's Griff suddenly so concerned for your safety? She let you go off on your own last time we were in town."

"Kingston's changed, and not for the better, since you was last in port," said one of the sailors. "Gangs we have now, roaming the streets. Bullies paid by Maleficious to stir up trouble. That little worm Rufius gives them their orders. He tells 'em who to target, who to lock up, who to kick like a dog." The sailor took his pipe out of his mouth and spat. "That Tarn, that imp of yours, he better watch himself. The gangs are going after imps, driving them out of town. Or worse."

A frown creased Krill's handsome dark face. "Maybe I'll go with you after all. Just til you reach the castle area, anyway. You'll be safe enough there, at least in daylight."

Krill shook hands with a sailor and passed him what looked to Nikki like some kind of paper money, folded into a little square. The sailor tucked it into a pocket and went back to mending his net. Krill strode rapidly down the dock, his long legs covering distance so fast that Nikki, Kira, and Curio had to jog to keep up with him.

The dockyards of Kingston were busy with sailing ships and barges criss-crossing the harbor and pulling up to its wharves. Nikki saw far more than fish being unloaded onto the docks. Barrels smelling of wine and beer were rolled down gangplanks. Wooden crates smelling of pepper, cloves, nutmeg, and oranges were loaded onto carts pulled by donkeys. Bundles of cotton and wool were tossed by sunburned sailors into over-loaded wagons. Custom officials rushed around shouting orders to dockworkers and getting curses in return.

Nikki was so busy dodging rolling barrels, braying donkeys, and cursing sailors that she barely noticed that they had started to climb out of the port area. Krill was leading them up a steep cobblestoned street lined with warehouses and taverns. A muddy stream of water flowed in the gutter and piles of steaming donkey droppings attracted swarms of flies. The street was crowded with sailors staggering around singing loudly and smelling of stale beer.

Kira pointed at a wooden sign hanging in front of a tavern. A crude portrait of an old man with a long gray beard was painted on the sign. "Grays Inn," she said a little breathlessly as she jogged to keep up with Krill. "If we get separated just ask for directions to Grays Inn. Everyone in town knows it, even the courtiers. It brews the best beer in Kingston, so even the snobs up in the castle come down here for a pint."

Nikki nodded, taking a quick glance around, trying to remember landmarks so she could find the inn again if she had to. Next to the inn rose a giant oak tree. Horses stood in its shade, munching on piles of hay. It was the only tree on the street so Nikki was pretty sure she'd remember it.

As she jogged along behind Kira Nikki tried to formulate a plan. She couldn't just walk up to the castle and announce herself. Maleficious might be there, and she had no desire to get thrown into anymore castle dungeons. The problem was, she didn't have any other ideas. Her original plan, ever since Curio had led her into the Trackless Forest, had been to get to the Southern Castle. The castle was where Athena was headed and Nikki very much wanted to find Athena and Fuzz. Griff and Kira had been very nice to her, but they were new acquaintances. Athena and Fuzz felt like old friends by comparison and Nikki very much wanted to be around familiar faces right now. The frightening feeling of being unanchored, lost in a strange land, was much stronger when she wasn't with Athena and Fuzz. And the large crowded city of Kingston made the feeling worse. Nikki could feel panic just under the surface or her outward calm. She was trying to ignore it, to stuff it down, but it wouldn't go away. Part of the reason Athena and Fuzz made her feel secure was that they knew how to get her back home. Back through the portal near Castle Cogent. Back to her Mom, her school, and her own world.

Nikki's first thought on landing in Kingston had been to rush up to the castle. She'd caught a glimpse of it as they sailed into port. It was a forbidding-looking fortress, perched high above the city on a rocky bluff. High stone walls surrounded it and soldiers in flashing armor patrolled the walls. She hadn't liked the look of it. It was much more of a military fortress than Castle Cogent. Castle Cogent had white marble walls, purple banners, and gardens with peacocks wandering on green lawns. If Castle Cogent was Sleeping Beauty then the Southern Castle was the Wicked Witch. But the Southern Castle was where Athena and Fuzz had been headed, so that was where she had to go. But now that she was here in Kingston obvious difficulties presented themselves. Would they even let her into the castle? What if Athena and Fuzz were still wandering somewhere in the Trackless Forest? She glanced at Curio jogging beside her. She couldn't risk Curio getting arrested. She could ask Kira to look after him while she went up to the castle alone, but somehow she didn't think Curio would go along with that idea.

"Hold on a second," said Krill, coming to an abrupt halt. "There's a carriage coming down the hill. It's a real tight corner here. We don't want to get squashed. Get back against the wall." He scrunched them against the tall stone wall that bordered the street.

Nikki couldn't see the carriage but she could hear it. The hooves of the horses sounded like thunder on the cobblestones of the steep street. There was a sharp bend in the road and as Nikki peered around it the first horse appeared, a headdress of purple feathers sprouting between its ears. The carriage the horse was pulling was very wide, so wide that it barely managed to maneuver around the corner without scraping its gilded sides on the stone wall. Purple velvet curtains hid the occupants inside. Up top a coachman in a black satin coat and breeches sat behind the horses, cracking his whip and shouting at a drunken sailor to get out of the way.

"Halt!"

The command had come from inside the carriage. As the horses slowed to a stop, stamping their hooves impatiently, a pale hand pulled aside the velvet curtain and a dark-haired man looked out.

The hair on Nikki's neck stood up. It was Rufius.

"Well!" said Rufius. "This is a pleasant surprise." He opened the carriage door and climbed out, carefully avoiding the muddy stream of water running down the gutter. He was dressed in his usual spotless black tunic and sandals. His cave-dweller pale skin seemed to glow in the shadow of the high stone wall. He crossed his arms and surveyed Nikki and her companions. "You'll have to introduce me to your friends," he said. "You've taken on some unfamiliar acquaintances. The last time I saw you you were in the company of those two extremely annoying King's emissaries. Where are they, by the way? I'd like to have a little chat with them."

Nikki just glared at him.

"Look, sir," said Krill, his tone halfway between polite and angry. "We have no business with you. We'll just be on our way." He shooed the others in front of him and tried to continue up the hill.

Rufius whistled and a coachman who'd been riding on the back of the carriage suddenly stepped in front of them, blocking the way.

Krill's hands formed into fists. "Get out of my way, sir, if you know what's good for you."

Kira laid a hand on Krill's arm just as Rufius made a sudden grab at Curio. Curio dodged just in time and squirmed under the carriage. Fast as a cobra Rufius changed course and tried to grab Nikki. Krill's long arm lashed out and shoved Rufius to the ground. The coachman rushed forward but Krill's fist smashed against his jaw and knocked him reeling against the stone wall.

"Run!" shouted Krill.

Curio scrambled out from under the carriage and they all dashed up the hill.

Rufius shouted at the coachman Krill had punched to follow

them, but the coachman was staggering around in dizzy circles holding his head.

As they rounded the sharp corner Nikki glanced back. Rufius was yelling at the coachman on top of the carriage to get down. The coachman, gray-haired and paunchy, was slowly climbing down from his perch. No threat there, Nikki thought. The coachman that Krill had punched was now vomiting in the gutter and Rufius showed no sign of trying to follow them on his own. Probably too scared of Krill, she thought. Rufius was a bully, but like most bullies he had a cowardly streak. For the first time since she'd arrived in the Realm of Reason she was glad of the lack of technology in the Realm. Back home in Wisconsin Rufius would have just called the police on his cell phone and Nikki and her friends would have been arrested before they'd gone another block. Nikki was sure there were plenty of soldiers up at the castle ready to jump into action when Rufius gave an order, but they were far out of shouting range. And she doubted that Rufius could convince any of the sailors they'd passed to follow them. Most of the sailors were far too drunk to be any use to him, and from what she'd heard down on the docks the sailors couldn't stand Rufius anyway.

Krill, who was far ahead of the others, turned and waited for them, beckoning them into an alleyway next to a warehouse full of sheepskins. The hill was very steep, and when Nikki, Kira, and Curio reached him they leaned against the rough wooden wall of the warehouse, breathing hard.

"We have to get off the street," gasped Kira. "Go back to the ship."

Krill shook his head. "No, this is serious trouble. We can't bring it down on Griff's head. Rufius has enough power here in Kingston to throw the whole crew into the castle dungeon." He eyed Nikki. "Just what is it he wants with you?"

"I don't think he really wants me," said Nikki. "He's trying to capture Fuzz and Athena, the two imps I've been travelling with. They seem to be leaders among the imps. And they're close to the King, so they're a threat to Maleficious and Rufius."

Krill nodded slowly, rubbing the hand he'd punched the coachman with. He glanced up over their heads at the castle walls, a section of which could be seen from the alley. "Haven't seen the King's flag flying today. It's a big purple banner with a gold crown on it. Hard to miss. You can see it all the way down at the docks. They fly it from the tallest tower of the castle when the King's in residence. If it's not flying that used to mean that the King's not here. He's at Castle Cogent. But I've been hearing strange things from the sailors on the docks. They say that Maleficious and Rufius have gained power over the King. That he leaves the running of Kingston to them while he wastes time entertaining his courtiers. He neglects his duties to the people of the Realm." He frowned up at the castle again. "So, I'm not sure we can trust the flag. The King might be here in Kingston, or he might not. Maleficious may have ordered that the flag not be flown, even if the King's in residence. That would keep the people of the city in the dark. If anyone wanted to petition the King, to complain about how Maleficious and Rufius are throwing their weight around, they wouldn't be able to tell if the King was here."

Nikki bit her lip. She'd been counting on the King being here at the Southern Castle. Athena had been so sure he'd be here. The plan she'd been hastily concocting as she ran up the hill away from Rufius had been to find the King and ask for his protection. If Fuzz and Athena weren't here in Kingston her second best option was to find the King. She was pretty sure he'd help her. He'd been very nice to her back at Castle Cogent. Of course, he'd also been very nice to Maleficious, which was discouraging. Still, it was the best plan she could come up with. "I think I should go up to the castle, flag or no flag. I can ask one of the guards if the King is in residence."

Kira gasped. "You'll be arrested on the spot."

"I don't think so," said Nikki. "The King knows me. I met him a few weeks ago, when Fuzz and Athena brought me through the . . ." She hesitated. Kira and Krill knew she was a stranger, but she wasn't sure how they would react to the news that she had come through a portal from another world. "Through the gates of Castle Cogent. The King was very nice and we talked for quite a while in his garden. I'm sure he'll remember me."

Kira and Krill both shook their heads vigorously.

"A year ago that might have worked," said Krill. "The Head Guard up at the castle would have taken a message to the King and you might have been admitted inside the walls. The King has always been very relaxed about security. He likes to talk to his subjects, something I've always admired about him. But a year ago Maleficious was just the King's advisor and no one had heard of Rufius. As far as anyone knew the King was still in charge. Still leader of the Realm. I don't think that's the case anymore. If you go up to the castle the guards will hold you until they can ask Maleficious or Rufius what to do with you."

Nikki slumped against the warehouse wall. Now she had no idea what to do or where to go. She badly wished Athena and Fuzz were here to advise her. Or better yet, said a small childish voice in her head, maybe she should give up all this tramping about the Realm. Maybe she should head back to Castle Cogent and go back through the portal to her own world. This world and its problems were really none of her concern.

Nikki blushed with guilt at thinking such a thing. Athena and Fuzz were her friends, and they were in trouble. They had come all the way from another world to the janitor's closet at her high school to seek her assistance. It would have been better if they'd chosen someone else from her world. A powerful person, like a politician or a scientist. Or at least a grown-up. But they had chosen her and she couldn't just abandon them.

"Well," said Kira, "if we can't go back to the ship and we can't go up to the castle then there's only one thing to do. We'll go to see the Prince."

"Hmm," said Krill, weighing this idea. "Do you think he'd hide us?"

Kira nodded. "I'm sure he would. But he might not need to. If we can get to his mansion we'll be under his protection. His guests. The Prince has a lot of power here in Kingston, almost as much as the King himself. Even Rufius would think twice before crossing the Prince."

Chapter Six

The Prince Of Physics

"THE PRINCE IS at dinner, Miss. He is entertaining guests from the Western Isles. He can't just abandon them. It would be the height of rudeness." The Head Butler brushed a miniscule piece of dust from his green satin tailcoat and turned away. The footman who had let them in opened the front door and gestured for them to leave.

They were standing in the marble foyer of the mansion belonging to the Prince of Physics. The black and white tiled floor was so polished Nikki could see her reflection in it. In front of her a grand marble staircase swept up in graceful curves to the second floor. To her left was a glass-enclosed room that looked like an elegant greenhouse. Nikki could see potted palms, orange trees, ferns, orchids, and other plants she didn't recognize. The glass room had a dramatic view over the city of Kingston and its harbor. Night had fallen and torches flickered along the main streets of the city. A full moon shone down on the ships in the harbor. Nikki wondered if Griff had any of her crew out looking for them. Probably. It was long past the time they were supposed to meet back at Grays Inn.

They would have arrived at the Prince's mansion much sooner if it hadn't been for the patrols. Rufius had obviously given orders for the soldiers up at the castle to find them. They'd spotted many of these search parties on the streets, each consisting of five soldiers in full armor. The search parties were certainly intimidating, but also surprisingly ineffective. Five soldiers in clanking armor made a lot of noise. As soon as they heard the clank of metal echoing off the cobblestones Krill herded them into an alley or behind a cluster of bushes. The soldiers hadn't been able to find them but the patrols had made it difficult for them to move through the city. They'd spent hours dashing through Kingston's back streets, dodging and hiding.

"This is ridiculous," said Kira, glaring at the retreating Head Butler. "Once the Prince realizes how serious the situation is he'll be glad to help us. No pompous lackey in a pea-green coat is going to stop me from seeing him." She dodged the footman who was trying to herd them outside and dashed up the sweeping marble staircase.

The Head Butler gasped in surprise as she ran past him. He put a hand out to stop her, but Kira was much too fast for him. She reached the second floor before he'd gone another step.

Krill shook his head, a small smile breaking out on his handsome face. "She's a hard one to stop when she wants something, is Kira. Well, I guess we'd better follow her."

"Do you know the Prince too?" asked Nikki as she followed him up the staircase.

"No," said Krill. "Never met the chap. I only got a brief glimpse of him once, when he came aboard our ship last year. He's some kind of distant relation to Griff. But she didn't introduce him to the rest of the crew. Kira knows him cause of that fancy instrument, that sextant she's always fooling around with. She tried to teach me how to use it, but I couldn't get my thoughts around it. Too complicated. I leave that fancy stuff to her. Give me a net to haul and a dice game in the evening and I'm happy. Anyway, she's been here to the Prince's mansion half a dozen times, usually with Griff. The Prince likes to talk to her about his inventions. Not many people understand them, so I guess it's nice to have a chat with someone like Kira. Not that she understands everything he says, of course. He's spent his whole life around books and scholars. There's a rumor he has more than ten thousand books here in his mansion. Probably read them all, too. Kira and me, we haven't had much in the way of book-learning. Spent most of our lives at sea, and sailors aren't exactly known for their scholarly ways."

Krill fell silent as they reached the Prince's dining room. It was a huge room, with flashing chandeliers, tapestries on the walls, a fireplace big enough to stand in, a beautiful mural of a sunrise painted on the ceiling, and a polished walnut table at least fifty feet long. The silk curtains at the windows were open, showing the night sky full of stars.

Twenty people were seated at the table, dressed in silks and satins, with the men in frock coats and the ladies in long evening gowns. The jewels in the ladies hair sparkled in the light from the chandeliers. A swan made out of puff pastry sat in the middle of the table, swimming in a pool of sauce which smelled delightfully of oranges and honey. The guests were ladling the sauce over plates of fluffy meringue.

At the head of the table sat the Prince. Nikki studied him as he listened to Kira whispering in his ear. He was about her Mom's age, quite tall, surprisingly fit and athletic looking. After Krill's description she'd expected him to be a small stooped person, bent and nearsighted from peering at books all day. He had dark blonde hair, a long thin nose, and a vivid red mark on one cheek which reminded Nikki of the burns she'd seen on Gwen's arms. The results of Gwen's experiments with chemicals in her laboratory.

Nikki, Krill, and Curio had been hovering uncomfortably in the doorway, uncertain whether to enter. The Prince glanced up and waved them inside.

"Morton, bring in a few more chairs for our guests. There's a good fellow," said the Prince to the startled Head Butler who was standing behind them, puffing from having run up the stairs.

Morton looked like he wanted very much to object, but he did as the Prince asked, fetching a chair from the next room and personally seating Nikki at the table. A footman carried in two chairs for Krill and Curio.

The Prince motioned for the man seated at his left to move down a place so that Kira could sit next to him. The man's eyebrows raised up to his hairline, but he complied.

A footman served Nikki a plate of the meringue with orange sauce. Despite the fact that all the people at the table were staring at them Nikki couldn't help taking up a spoon and trying the dessert. The smell was impossible to resist, and it tasted even better. She'd never had meringue before. It was kind of like a big, chewy marshmallow. Next to her Curio was gobbling his down at lightning speed. A footman placed another helping in front of him and he disposed of that one just as fast.

The Prince laughed. "I see your young friend knows a good dish when he tastes one. I'll inform my chef that his Clouds in an Orange Sea is a success."

The guests at the table began digging into their desserts again, and the small talk around the table resumed. After dessert the footmen passed around cups of tea with crunchy cinnamon cookies. Nikki politely took a cup and two of the cookies. Curio turned his nose up at the tea but grabbed a handful of cookies and wolfed them down.

Nikki saw the Prince watching Curio. The Prince had a brief word with one of the footmen, and a few minutes later full plates were placed in front of her, Curio, Kira, and Krill. Nikki tucked into the plate of chicken in gravy, mashed potatoes, dumplings, and green beans with gusto. They hadn't eaten since leaving the ship early that morning. The nerve-wracking experience of hiding from the patrols of soldiers had left no time to think about food, but now that a full plate was in front of her she realized how hungry she was. She joined Curio in eagerly accepting seconds when the footman at her elbow held out a platter with more chicken and dumplings.

After cleaning her plate except for one drumstick Nikki removed her rucksack and checked inside. Cation was snoozing on top of a woolen scarf Kira had lent Nikki. The kitten had a remarkable ability to sleep through just about anything. Nikki tucked the drumstick in front of Cation's nose. The kitten yawned widely and sleepily nibbled at the chicken. Nikki placed the rucksack on the floor and leaned back in her chair, hands folded over her comfortably full stomach. Now that she was fed and in a relatively safe place Kingston suddenly didn't seem like such a scary city. She was just wondering if the Prince might offer them a bed for the night, when loud voices from down in the foyer broke into her thoughts.

The talk around the table ceased and the Prince stood up, frowning. "What new interruption is this?" he asked as Morton the Head Butler rushed into the room.

"My lord, the Regent is downstairs," said Morton. "He requires a word with you."

"He requires more than a word," said Rufius, strolling into the dining room. He was wearing a long black cloak over his usual tunic. A small crown woven out of gold thread decorated the neck of the cloak. Out in the hallway a rumble of metallic clanks could be heard. A patrol of soldiers marched into the dining room and lined up against the wall, their spears pointing up at the ceiling.

The Prince's face turned red with anger. "How dare you bring armed soldiers into my home," he said through clenched teeth. "Remove them at once."

Rufius laughed, snatching up a cookie from a guest's plate and calmly eating it while staring at the Prince. "The last time I checked, my lord, you were not in charge of the King's guard."

"Nor are you," said the Prince. "And the last time *I* checked you were just a minion of that power-hungry old fool, Maleficious. Regent? Is that some new title you have assigned yourself?"

"Actually, the King bestowed it on me," said Rufius. "He felt I needed a more official designation, to help me in my duties."

The Prince snorted. "And do these duties include barging into a private home while the owner is entertaining guests?"

"Yes," said Rufius. "Especially when these guests are outlaws who have broken the laws of the Realm. I have orders to take them up to the castle for interrogation."

Krill jumped up, his hands clenched, but the Prince waved him back down.

"I will need to see a written order signed by the King, listing these so-called crimes," said the Prince. "I presume you have such a thing with you."

Rufius's eyes flashed dangerously. "As Regent I am not in need of such a document."

"As a member of the King's Council I say that you are," said the Prince. He nodded to Morton. The Head Butler stepped out into the hall and whistled. Twenty footmen filed into the dining room, each armed with a long wooden pole. They lined up in front of the soldiers, their poles pointing at he soldiers' feet.

Nikki guessed that the footmen were going to try to trip the soldiers and grab their spears, but she hoped it wouldn't come to that. The spear tips looked horribly sharp and some of the soldiers were also carrying swords. She didn't want anyone getting hurt on her account. She was the only one in the room Rufius really wanted. She was just rising from her chair, with the idea of turning herself in, when Rufius gave a disgusted snort and waved dismissively at the soldiers. They filed out of the room, their metal leg-coverings clanking loudly on the marble staircase.

Rufius glared at the Prince. "You're playing a dangerous game, my lord," he said. "Power in the Realm has shifted and you are on the weaker side."

The Prince shrugged. "Weak or strong, it matters not to me. I will always be on the side which opposes tyranny and power-hungry fools such as yourself."

Rufius's pale skin turned even paler, and for a second it looked like he was going to strike the Prince. But his clenched hand lowered and he abruptly turned and left the room.

Sighs of relief went around the table. The Prince's dinner guests rose as one and made quick excuses about having other parties to go to that evening. They all hurried out after a quick bow or curtsey to the Prince.

"Well," said the Prince, eyeing Kira. "That was certainly an unexpected addition to the evening. What have you been up to since I last saw you? Stealing the King's jewels?"

Kira laughed nervously. "No, my lord. We have committed no crimes. But we have fallen out of favor with Rufius. A dangerous state to be in."

"Indeed," said the Prince. "Well, regardless, you will have to stay here tonight. I can't very well send you back to your ship. You'll be snatched up at spear-point before you've left my gardens." He signaled to the Head Butler. "It's getting late. We'll discuss this in the morning. Morton will show you to your rooms."

RUNNING WATER. NIKKI stared in amazement as cold water rushed out of the pipe and flowed into a porcelain bowl. It was morning and Nikki was in the bedroom the Head Butler had assigned her. She was wrapped in a woolen robe which smelled faintly of lavender and on her feet were comfy felt slippers. The night before she'd been too tired to do anything but crawl into bed, but this morning she'd searched the room for a chamber pot like the one she'd used at Castle Cogent. She hadn't found any chamber pots, but to her surprise the bedroom had an actual bathroom attached to it. With actual plumbing.

She turned off the tap, still shaking her head. Nowhere else in the Realm had she seen this level of technology. There was a sink, the porcelain bowl she'd just filled, and even a toilet. It didn't look like the ones back in Wisconsin, but there was no mistaking its purpose. Nikki pulled on a long metal chain which hung from the ceiling and watched as the contents of the toilet flushed down a pipe.

"Pretty wild, huh?" she said to Cation, who was curled up on the white tiles of the bathroom floor, gnawing on the drumstick from last night's dinner. Cation looked up at her in a bored sort of way and went back to her drumstick.

"Well, *I* think it's pretty amazing," said Nikki. "I had no idea there was plumbing anywhere in the Realm. All I've seen so far is chamber pots and out-houses." She peered closely at the curved pewter handle of the tap over the sink. "I wonder how the water gets into the mansion." She was kneeling down for a closer look at the pipe coming out of the toilet when a knock sounded on the bedroom door.

"Morning," chirped Kira, bounding into the room when Nikki opened the door. "It's a lovely day. I'd take you up the hill and show you the Public Gardens if you weren't such a dangerous outlaw. Kind of puts a crimp in the sightseeing plans when your guest might be arrested at any moment." She dropped two cloth bags on Nikki's bed. "Clean clothes," she said, opening the larger bag and pulling out Nikki's jeans, underwear, socks, and Westlake Debate Team T-shirt. All freshly laundered. Even Nikki's muddy Nikes were spotless. And the torn sole had been repaired.

Kira flopped down on the bed. "Wouldn't mind living here all the time," she said. "Having someone else do all the laundry and the cooking. Course, on the Sunfish Posie does most of the cooking, though the rest of us have to help peel potatoes and gut fish."

Nikki went into the bathroom to change and came back feeling like she was in the wrong century. She plucked at her T-shirt. "Um, aren't I going to stick out a bit, in these clothes? I'd like to blend in more, especially since Rufius wants to arrest me."

Kira nodded and dug into the bag again. "That hooded overshirt you had on was full of rips and holes. Beyond repair was how the Prince's seamstress put it. She made you this." She handed Nikki a dark blue silk tunic.

Nikki pulled it on over her head and tied the matching belt. The tunic hung to her knees and had delicate sky-blue embroidery around the neckline. "It's lovely," she said. "But it looks expensive. I'm not sure I should accept something I can't pay for."

Kira waived away her concerns. "The Prince is one of the richest people in the Realm. He's not going to miss a bit of cloth." She opened the other bag. "Breakfast," she said, pulling out a basket full of scones, a pot of jam, some hard-boiled eggs and a wedge of cheese. "Krill's already eaten. He's gone out with a few of the Prince's men to see what's going on. The good news is that the Prince's mansion isn't surrounded by soldiers. The bad news is that we're trapped here until we can find out what Rufius is planning. There may not be soldiers lined up in the garden, but you can bet that Rufius has spies planted nearby, waiting to follow us when we leave."

Nikki spread jam on a scone. "What about Curio?"

"Sound asleep," said Kira. "Poor wee little tyke was tuckered out. Plus I think he ate a whole chicken last night." She looked up from the hard-boiled egg she was peeling. "Not any of my business, I know, but he seems a strange sort of travelling companion. Aren't his parents wondering where he is?"

"He doesn't have any parents," said Nikki. "He's an orphan. A pedestal baby."

"Oh," said Kira, shaking her head sadly. "That Deceptionville custom. We've heard of it, even here in Kingston. Seems barbaric. But then a lot of what I hear of Deceptionville seems barbaric. Kingston has its problems, but at least we don't leave poor wee little babes on stone pillars. What if no one claims them? Do they just starve? Here in Kingston we have the foundling home. Mothers who can't care for their babies leave them at the foundling home. It's not an easy life, being a foundling, but at least they're fed and housed. Get a bit of education too. A lot of the foundlings end up as servants to rich people, like the Prince. Not the worst thing that could happen to you."

Kira frowned, tracing a pattern on the coverlet of the bed with her finger. Nikki wondered if she was thinking of her own childhood, taken from her parents by pirates when she was only six and sold into slavery. Nikki was going to ask her if she wanted to talk about it, when Kira suddenly jumped up.

"Well, we can't stay here all day lazing about. I'll show you around the mansion. It's quite a place."

"Let's start with the plumbing," said Nikki, wiping scone crumbs off her hands. "I want to see how the water gets into the bathroom."

Kira laughed. "You sound just like me. I thought it was some sort of strange sorcery when I first turned one of those taps. The whole thing is quite complicated. It's the Prince's own invention. C'mon. We'll need to go out into the gardens. That's where the source of the water is."

They walked quietly through the grand halls of the mansion, occasionally passing a footman carrying linen or a tray of food. No one was in the black and white tiled foyer. At the front entrance Kira paused, peering out through a piece of glass inset in the massive front door.

"I don't see anyone about," she said. "No one dangerous looking, anyway. Just a few gardeners and some footmen out by the hedges, watching the street. The Prince must have told them to keep watch. It should be safe enough if we keep close to the house."

They slipped out the door and Kira led Nikki down a garden path bordered by salmon-pink roses. The Prince's gardens were extensive, nearly a quarter mile wide, Nikki guessed. They were laid out along several wide terraces overlooking the sea. The formal flower gardens were on the lower level in front of the mansion. Paths covered in crushed white stone meandered through rose and lilac bushes. At the center was a huge bronze fountain with a pod of dolphins leaping in jets of water.

They climbed a flight of stone steps to the second level and passed under a trellis dripping with purple Wisteria blossoms. Another flight of steps and they were at the top of the gardens. Nikki could see the flags of the castle waving high above her. At her feet was a swift-rushing stream that flowed down from the pine-covered slopes between the mansion and the King's castle. The rushing stream had been re-directed into a little stone-sided canal only two feet wide. Kira led her uphill along the canal until they came to a waterwheel. The water of the canal rushed into a wooden chute suspended over the waterwheel. The water dropped from the chute onto the top of the waterwheel and struck its wooden slats, turning the wheel on a wooden axle. Attached to the axle was a complex contraption which Nikki couldn't make sense of.

Kira laughed. "Quite a sight, isn't it? I looked just as confused as you, the first time I saw it. Took a lot of explaining before I understood it. Fortunately the Prince likes to explain his inventions." She pointed at the top of the wheel, where the water hit it. "The water is the power, of course. It runs downhill with quite a bit of force and pushes the wheel, which turns on this axle." She hopped over the little canal and Nikki followed.

Kira pointed at a wooden gear which was turned by the rotating axle of the waterwheel. "Watch that gear. See how its little cogs catch the cogs on the gear next to it? That converts the power from horizontal to vertical. The second gear pushes this long pole up and down. See the bucket attached to the pole? Watch, it's coming back down."

As Nikki watched the bucket dipped into a pool of water at the bottom of the waterwheel, filled with water, and travelled back up as the pole was pushed by the turning gear. When the bucket reached the top of the pole it tipped its water into a wooden chute which ran along a high stone wall. Then as the waterwheel kept turning the gears turned again and brought the bucket back down to repeat the process.

Kira pointed at the stone wall. "It runs all the way to the house. See? The chute is like a little river on top of the wall. The other end of the chute empties into that big wooden tank on the roof of the house. There are pipes running down from the tank, a big one for the kitchen and smaller ones for each bathroom. When you turn the tap in your bathroom a valve opens and lets the water flow down from the tank on the roof."

Nikki nodded. Once the system was explained it wasn't that hard to understand. She knew from a school trip to the Alexander Hydroelectric Dam on the Wisconsin River that the chute suspended above the waterwheel was called a penstock. The wheel itself worked the same way as the turbines in a modern dam, taking the kinetic energy of the falling water and converting that energy into mechanical energy which turned the gears attached to the wheel's axle. She peered up at the top of the wheel. The chute the water flowed down was suspended nearly five feet above the top of the wheel, to take advantage of gravity. The farther the water fell the more kinetic energy it had when it hit the slats of the wheel. The power of the falling water was directly proportional to the distance it fell. If the chute had been raised twice as high, say ten feet above the wheel instead of five, then the power it generated would be twice as much.

The output chute which ran along the top of the wall was just a smaller version of a Roman aqueduct. She'd seen pictures of these in her World History class. The Roman empire had built them two thousand years ago. They were long stone structures which looked like arched bridges and sometimes ran for miles. They had a narrow canal either on top or inside the structure which transported water from a distant source like a lake or a spring. Cities such as Nimes and Rome had been able to grow quite large due to this artificial source of water.

Nikki turned her attention to the bucket going up and down with the long pole. It couldn't hold much water, only about half a gallon per trip. "An Archimedes screw would be much more efficient," she said, thinking aloud.

"A what?" asked Kira.

Nikki bit her lip. Here she was again, back in the tricky area of trying to figure out which technology the Realm might or might not have. Archimedes screws were probably safe to discuss, she decided. They were extremely old technology in her world, having been invented by the Greek scientist and mathematician Archimedes around 300 BC. Some historians thought they'd been used in the Middle East even earlier. It was pretty likely that an inventor in the Realm had already experimented with them. If not the Prince then maybe someone like Gwen. And Archimedes screws couldn't be turned into weapons the way gunpowder could. At least she hoped not. Nikki sighed. This balancing act between two worlds was giving her a headache.

"An Archimedes screw is kind of what it sounds like," said Nikki. "It's a big screw made out of wood or metal. It pulls water from a lower source, like the canal here, to an upper source, like the chute on top of the wall. It would replace the bucket you have here. It could move more water than the bucket can. Though, now that I think about it, maybe that's not a good thing. I suppose it could fill the tank on the roof too fast. If the tank overflowed the roof of the mansion could collapse."

Kira wasn't to be put off by collapsing roofs. "How does this screw thing work?"

Nikki hunted on the ground until she found a short stick. She cleared a patch of dirt under a lilac bush and drew a circle with a smaller circle next to it. "I'm not much of an artist, but pretend this is your waterwheel and the small circle is the gear attached to its axle."

She drew a long rectangular box attached to the gear and going up at a steep angle. "The Archimedes screw is inside this box. As I said, it's just a big screw, which is a helix wrapped around a pole." She drew spirals going up inside the box. "When the axle of the waterwheel turns it turns the gear which turns the screw. The bottom of the screw is inside the pool of water at the bottom of your waterwheel. The top of the screw would go up to the chute on top of the stone wall. When the screw turns the water gets trapped on the first turning of the spiral and travels along the length of the screw inside the box. Then when it gets to the top of the screw it pours out into the chute. Then the chute would carry the water to the house, as it's doing now."

Kira knelt down and frowned at the drawing in the dirt. "I've seen screws before, but never one as big as what you're describing. But I kind of see what you mean." She pointed at the box with the spirals in it. "What is this for? I mean, wouldn't the water travel up the screw anyway? Why does the screw have to be inside a box?"

"The box keeps the water from splashing over the edge of the spirals," said Nikki. "You're right, some of the water would travel up to the top of the screw even without the box. But the box keeps the water from going all over the place. More water reaches the top." She drew another picture in the dirt, this one a long tube with spirals inside. "It doesn't have to be a rectangular box. A long wooden or metal cylinder would work even better, since it's closer to the shape of the screw."

Kira was about to ask another question when they both fell silent. A crunch of gravel could be heard just below them. Someone was coming up the hill.

Kira grabbed Nikki's arm and pulled her behind the lilac bush. They crouched down, peering through the leaves.

"Kira?" said a voice only a few feet away. "I know you're up here somewhere. Stop messing about."

Kira rolled her eyes and stepped out from behind the lilac bush.

"Over here," she said, waving at Krill as his head appeared at the top of the flight of stairs leading to the terrace.

Krill loped over to them, his long legs making short work of the hilly terrain. "What are you two doing out here by yourselves? Back to the house, right now."

Kira folded her arms, her face the very model of stubbornness. "You're suddenly very high and mighty, Mr. Bossy. Who are you to be throwing around orders as if you're the King himself?"

Krill sighed. "I'm just trying to keep you safe, you annoying little nitwit. Me and some of the Prince's men went into town and hung out in the Blackbird Tavern. Best place in town to pick up news. We heard a rumor that Rufius is trying to bribe some of the Prince's footmen. Get them to work for him. Don't know if any of them having taken the money, but it only takes one or two bad apples. They could snatch you right out of the garden here and have you locked up in the castle dungeon before you knew what was happening."

Kira dismissed this news with a contemptuous snort, but Nikki noticed that she didn't hesitate to follow Krill when he started back down the hill. They followed him down the terraces and back through the rose garden in front of the mansion. The Prince's footmen were still stationed along the outer hedges, watching the street, but now Nikki looked at them suspiciously, wondering if any of them were now working for Rufius. She breathed a sigh of relief when the massive front door of the mansion closed behind them.

Chapter Seven

The Knights of the Iron Fist

KRILL HERDED THEM into a parlor on the ground floor. "Stay in here where I can keep an eye on you," he said.

Nikki looked around at the silk curtains on the windows, the murals on the walls, and the crystal vases overflowing with vivid blue hydrangeas. The beautiful room seemed like a strange place to play dice, but that's exactly what the huddle of footmen crouched in the middle of the carpet were doing. Krill went over to join them while Kira and Nikki sat down in a window seat overlooking the rose garden.

"C'mon, you slimy eel," said a footman to Krill. "Get your bet in already."

"Got a tenner here that says you're deader than a speared tuna," Krill said calmly, laying a bill down on top of a pile of coins inside the huddle. "May as well leave the game now, Brenner. The dice have been loving me lately. They say down at the docks that I can't lose."

Brenner snorted, throwing a handful of coins onto the pile. "Oh, you'll lose all right. The odds are in my favor today."

Nikki watched the game, only mildly interested. Gambling had never appealed to her. There wasn't usually much skill or brains required to play games of chance, especially in the type of dice-throwing game the footmen were playing. They were throwing two dice on the floor, betting on which numbers would come up. They took turns throwing the dice. Two sixes coming up earned the thrower the most money. Two fours or two fives earned him a bit less. A different number on each of the dice meant no money was won or lost and the thrower tried again. Two ones coming up meant the dice thrower lost all of the money he'd put into the pile on the floor.

Krill took four turns throwing the dice and won each time, three times with two sixes. He had a large pile of bills and coins in front of him and was getting ready to throw again.

"Take the money and get out of the game, you stupid snorting walrus," whispered Kira, suddenly intent on the game. "That much money would buy the whole crew of the Sunfish some nice treats for a year," she said to Nikki. "We could get Posie some of the peppermint candies she loves. And Griff likes a nice bottle of wine now and then. We could surprise her with a top quality one from the Southern Isles."

They watched as Krill pulled a wrinkled wad of bills from his pocket and dropped them on the pile. He picked up the dice, closed his eyes, and threw.

Loud groans mixed with laughter came from the footmen. Krill had thrown two ones. His mouthed dropped open in disbelief. He sat staring at the dice as his lost money was divided up among the others.

"Hey, eel," said Brenner. "Place another bet or get your slimy carcass out of the ring."

Krill shook his head and stood up so slowly it looked like he'd turned into an old man. "Got no more money to bet with," he said.

Kira slapped her forehead with her palm. "Stupid, stupid, stupid. The fool's got no self control when it comes to dice. He says it's harmless fun. I say it's not when you can't control yourself every time you get in a game." She rolled her eyes as Krill walked over to them and flopped down on the carpet. He lay on his back and put his crossed arms over his face.

"But the dice were in my favor," he said. "In my favor. I'd rolled sixes, three times in four throws. The next roll should've been sixes again. I've been rolling nothing but sixes down at the ducks."

The gamblers fallacy, thought Nikki, sighing. Even smart people fell for it. It took various forms. Usually the gambler insisted that a bad run of cards or dice was about to turn to his advantage. If he'd been throwing all ones then he was certain he was due to roll sixes on the next throw. In Krill's case he was insisting that the dice should have kept on doing what they had been, turning up sixes. Both versions were completely wrong. There was no "should" when it came to games of chance. In a game like Blackjack, where an expert card-counter could figure out the odds to some extent, then sometimes the player could predict the next hand. But in a completely random game like dice throwing each toss of the dice was independent of all other tosses. Just because you'd had an unusual streak, say throwing ones twenty times in a row, that didn't mean that the odds were somehow going to balance out by turning up sixes on the next throw. Her math teacher had explained it to her by using a coin toss. There were two possible outcomes of each coin toss: heads or tails. The probability of getting heads on one toss was fifty percent, or one in two. The probability of getting heads again on the next toss was still fifty percent. Even if you tossed the coin one hundred times and got heads each time, the probability of getting heads on the next toss was still fifty percent. Past tosses didn't affect future tosses in the slightest. You started over again with the same odds on each toss.

The gamblers fallacy reminded Nikki of Benedict the hermit and his insistence that everything happened for a reason. Just as Benedict was sure that the universe was watching out for him and pulling invisible strings to make his life turn out for the best, Krill was sure those same invisible strings were somehow controlling the dice he threw. The two fallacies were a combination of egotism and wishful thinking. Nikki couldn't imagine being so egotistical that you thought the entire universe was somehow obsessed with your tiny little life. She supposed it was comforting to think that way, but she preferred an accurate view of reality to a comforting one. The accurate view of reality was that there were no invisible strings, no mysterious force in the universe which was watching out for you. If you wanted to turn life in your favor then you had to buckle down and do some hard work.

Nikki was startled out of her thoughts by the sudden arrival of an out-of-breath footman. He ran into the parlor and waved frantically at the dice throwers to stop their game. Everyone waited while he gasped for breath.

"Knights!" he finally squeaked out. "The Knights of the Iron Fist! They've ridden into town. The whole lot of 'em."

Brenner pocketed his winnings and raised a skeptical eyebrow. "All of 'em? That's a whole lot of knights. Are you sure? Maybe someone is pulling your leg."

The footman shook his head. "Saw 'em with my own eyes. I was crossing Falder's Meadow when I saw 'em. My Jenny lives on the edge of the meadow. I was bringing her some cinnamon twists from the bakery when I nearly stumbled right into the middle of their camp. They've set up tents and everything. Rows and rows of tents. Looks like they're planning a long stay."

Nikki glanced from the footman to Kira to Krill. Everyone looked worried, but no one looked like they knew what to do. She'd encountered the Knights of the Iron Fist twice before, once in the Haunted Hills and then again at the headquarters of the imps. Neither encounter had been very pleasant. Nikki frowned, thinking back to the incident in the Haunted Hills. At first she'd thought the knights were good guys. They'd attacked the Confounded Castle, trying to drive out the Sorcerer who'd been frightening the local population with fake witchcraft and scary hooded figures on the castle's battlements. The Sorcerer had turned out to be Fortuna the Fortunate, though Nikki hadn't learned that until much later.

After their unsuccessful attack on the Confounded Castle the knights had forced her, Fuzz, and Athena to leave the Haunted Hills, on the orders of Rufius. Their connection to Rufius was worrying, but the knights had been very polite to her, and they'd seemed reluctant to do as Rufius commanded. Nikki had gotten the impression that at least some of the knights were decent types. But then there had been the very scary attack on the headquarters of the imps, with the knights setting fires at the entrances to all the tunnels of the headquarters to drive the imps out with smoke. Good guys didn't do awful things like that.

Loud shouts suddenly came from out in the gardens. Everyone rushed to the windows. Nikki parted a silk curtain and peered out. The footmen who'd been keeping watch out by the hedges were running toward the mansion. Behind them a row of knights on horseback was riding through the rose garden, the sun glinting off their armor. Each knight wore a white linen tunic over his armor with a picture of a red fist on the chest. All of the knights had swords and long spears which stood upright in a leather cup attached to their stirrup. They rode right up to the front door, reining in their horses but staying in the saddle. Intimidation tactics, thought Nikki. The knights knew they were more frightening when mounted.

The knight who'd been in the lead dismounted and banged on the front door of the mansion with his heavy metal-covered fist.

Everyone in the parlor stood looking at each other in frozen confusion. Finally a footman ran out of the room and soon after the Prince's voice could be heard coming down the marble staircase and into the black and white tiled foyer.

"Knights, you say? Some party of messengers from the castle?" asked the Prince.

"No, my lord," said the footman. "These appear to belong to the order known as the Knights of the Iron Fist. We have heard news that they are camped outside of the city near Falder's Meadow."

Nikki heard the front door open and she edged toward the door of the parlor, keeping out of sight but getting close enough to hear what was being said. She was relieved that metallic footsteps weren't clanking across the foyer. The Prince hadn't let the knight inside.

"Well, this is a surprise," said the Prince. "I haven't met any of your order in many years. What, may I ask, are you and your brethren doing in our fair city of Kingston?"

"That is not something I am authorized to discuss, my lord," replied the knight. "I am not privy to the councils of our troop commanders. However, the reason for my appearance at your door is no secret. I am here to collect one of your guests. A young woman who is a known companion of outlaws. We have orders to arrest her and bring her to the castle."

"My, my," said the Prince. "The known companion of outlaws. That is quite a charge. Unfortunately there is no one here of that description. I can assure you that all of my guests are law-abiding citizens of the Realm."

Nikki heard a clank, as if a metal-covered boot had tried to step into the foyer.

"The girl I speak of is of average height, with long dark hair," said the knight. "She has an unusual accent. She is not a citizen of the Realm, as you put it, much less a law-abiding one. She travels with two imps, notorious leaders of the imp rebellion."

"A rebellion by the imps?" asked the Prince. "This is the first I've heard of such a thing. Not that I would blame them. Their treatment by those in power, especially in the last few years, has been unforgivable."

"You would be wise not to say such things, my lord," said the knight. "The powerful might take it as criticism of their rule."

"That is exactly how I intended it," said the Prince calmly. "Now, if you'll excuse me, I was in the middle of an experiment. A most delicate one involving the suspension of solids in a liquid."

Nikki heard the front door of the mansion close with a bang.

"Well, you seem to be making some dangerous enemies," said the Prince to Kira as he stepped into the parlor. He eyed Nikki. "You certainly don't look like an outlaw. Then again Kira here doesn't look like one of the Realm's most knowledgeable experts on navigation, though that's precisely what she is."

"Sir," said Nikki, "You've been very kind to let us stay here. I don't want to get you in trouble. Maybe I should turn myself in."

The Prince waved this away with an impatient motion of his hand. "Brave, but foolhardy. These knights have obviously joined forces with Rufius and Maleficious. They are intent on rounding up people who oppose them and their quest for power." He parted a curtain and gazed out of the window at the knights milling about his rose garden on horseback. "They seem content to stay outside the house, at least for the moment. I find this turn of events most disheartening. I used to know some of the members of this order back in my youth. They were hotheaded, bent on adventure in foreign lands, possibly not very bright, but mostly they were good-hearted. Back then they tried to defend the weak, not trample on them. To see them joining with Rufius in his oppression of the imps is most disappointing."

He turned away from the window. "Well, I suppose I shall have to put my experiment on hold. We will go up to the castle and have a word with the King."

Kira looked at him in disbelief and pointed out the window, where a horse was nibbling on a rose right under the windowsill. "My lord, the knights have your mansion surrounded. It will be impossible to just walk out your front door and up the streets to the castle."

The Prince just smiled. "There is more than one way to visit a King, my dear Kira. Now, go collect your belongings and your little companion. Meet me in the kitchens in half an hour."

Krill loped off up the stairs to the bedroom he'd been assigned while Nikki and Kira went to find Curio. As they expected he was no longer in bed, but neither was he in any of the public rooms of the mansion. They looked in the parlors, the library, the beautiful greenhouse room overlooking the sea, but he was nowhere to be found. Finally a footman suggested they look in the kitchens, and sure enough both Curio and Cation were there, curled up together on top of a pile of flour sacks. A stout, motherly-looking cook was feeding them blueberry muffins.

Curio waved at them with his mouth full of muffin. "Hello, Miss," he mumbled. "Lovely morning, isn't it?"

"Finish up, little man," said Kira. "We need to pack up and head off."

"I've got nothing to pack, Miss," said Curio. He pointed down at his feet, where Nikki's rucksack was leaning against the flour sacks. "I brought this down in case the kitty wanted to ride in it. There are some noisy hounds outside, near the chicken coop. Their barking was making her nervous."

Nikki shouldered her rucksack and picked up Cation, who looked overfed and sleepy, but not the least bit nervous. She scratched the kitten behind the ears and tucked her in the rucksack. "Well, I'm all packed," she said. "How about you?" she asked Kira.

Kira laughed. "Travel light, you do. As for me, all my worldly goods are in my cabin on the Sunfish."

The Prince strode into the kitchen, followed by Krill. "I see everyone is ready. Wonderful. Let us be off, then." He opened a creaking door next to a huge walk-in fireplace and led them into a pantry stocked to the ceiling with baskets of onions and potatoes, bags of flour, bottles of wine, and crates of fruit. The Prince stopped next to a pile of crates filled with apples. He motioned to Krill and together they lifted the crates and shoved them against the wall. On the spot where the crates had been a trap door was just visible in the dusty stone floor. The Prince pulled on an iron ring set into the floor and the trap door creaked open. He held it open while the others climbed down a rough wooden ladder which descended into the darkness under the floor.

After the Prince had climbed in and closed the trap door the darkness was complete. Nikki waved her hand in front of her nose, but couldn't see a thing. She stepped on something soft and gave a little gasp, afraid it was a mouse.

"Miss, that's my foot," whispered Curio.

"Sorry," said Nikki.

There was a rasping sound and a smell of sulfur. The Prince had lit a pitch-covered torch. He held this aloft and led the way along a solidly-built brick tunnel.

Nikki was relieved that unlike the tunnels in the imp headquarters she could walk upright in this one. The tunnel went steadily uphill, with flights of steps at the steepest sections. After they had gone what Nikki guessed was about half a mile the Prince suddenly came to a halt.

He put a finger to his lips. "Wait here and make no sound." He gestured for Krill to come with him and they disappeared around a bend in the tunnel, taking the light with them.

Nikki, Kira and Curio huddled together in the darkness. Cation poked her head out of Nikki's rucksack and mewed loudly, her tiny claws digging into Nikki's shoulder.

"Sssshh" hissed Kira as Nikki frantically pushed the kitten down into the sack, only to have her pop back up again, complaining louder than ever.

"Here, Miss," said Curio, "try this." He pushed a rather squished blueberry muffin into Nikki's hand.

Nikki broke off a piece and stuffed it in the kitten's mouth. At first Cation somehow managed to both growl and chew at the same time, but gradually she subsided back into the bottom of the rucksack, taking the chunk of muffin with her.

Footsteps padded down the tunnel toward them and Krill appeared carrying the torch. He waved at them to follow him. On the other side of the bend in the tunnel was a very long, steep flight of stone steps. Krill pointed at a rope which was strung along the wall. They grasped it and started to climb.

"Krill," whispered Nikki after only ten steps.

Krill, who was in the lead, turned and looked down at her.

Nikki pointed at Curio. The steps were very high. Even Nikki and Kira were having trouble climbing them. For Curio they were too much. Each step was as high as his waist. To climb he had to push himself up with his hands and flop onto his stomach like a seal flopping up onto a rock. Then he swung his legs up and did it all over again on the next step.

Krill nodded and climbed back down to them. He handed the torch to Kira and bent down so that Curio could climb onto his back.

Kira took the lead, holding the torch aloft with one hand and hauling herself up by the rope with the other.

Nikki was dripping with sweat by the time they reached the top. Now she knew how mountain climbers felt when they reached the top of the Matterhorn. Their exhausted breathing sounded like a giant bellows in the closed space of the tunnel.

The Prince was waiting for them at the top of the stairs, holding open an iron door. A faint glimmer of light came through it. He took the torch from Kira and dropped it on the stone floor, stamping on it to extinguish the flame.

The door led into a large circular room. Its stone walls curved up into a dome painted with silver stars. Small round windows covered with a layer of grime let in faint streams of sunlight. A cluttered mess of wooden benches, dusty tables, stacks of parchment, and instruments of unknown purpose filled the room. The cold air had the stale, musty smell of a place which hadn't been used in years.

The Prince hurried to a door opposite the one they had entered. He put his ear to it and stood a long time, listening.

"All clear," he finally said in a normal voice. "I believe we can talk freely here. This room hasn't been used for a very long time and it is far removed from the populated areas of the castle." He swept a hand towards the mysterious instruments. "This used to be my laboratory, back when the father of the present King was on the throne. I was just a lad at the time and living in the castle. When I came into my inheritance and moved to my family's ancestral home I had the tunnel built. I thought it might prove a useful shortcut to the castle in times of disturbance. Fortunately Kingston has been peaceful in recent times and I've never had to use the tunnel, until now."

He pulled a canvas tarp off a nearby table and shook it out, releasing a cloud of dust. "My apologies. I know the conditions are not the best. Make yourselves as comfortable as you can." He handed the tarp to Kira, who put it around her shoulders to ward off the chilliness of the stone room.

Nikki shook out another tarp and wrapped it around Curio. She found one for herself and threw it over her shoulders. As a cloud of dust settled over her a sneeze came from her rucksack. Cation emerged, shaking herself angrily. She jumped down from Nikki's shoulder and stalked across the flagstone floor, growling in displeasure.

The Prince laughed. "I don't believe we've met," he said, scooping up Cation and holding her at eye level.

Cation's ears laid back and she hissed, squirming in his grasp.

Curio rushed up and held out the last of his now very squished blueberry muffin. "Here, sir. It'll make the two of you fast friends, or at least keep you from getting scratched. Quite a tiger, she is. You should have seen her take on the ship's cat. An ugly old devil, he was, and twice her size, but Cation soon sent him packing."

Cation sniffed suspiciously at the piece of muffin the Prince held out to her, but finally condescended to nibble daintily at it, giving the occasional growl just to show who was in charge.

"My lord, shouldn't we go to the King at once?" asked Krill. "If the Knights of the Iron Fist invade your mansion it won't take them long to find the trap door in the pantry. They could be hurrying along the tunnel as we speak."

Nikki, Kira and Curio all stared at the iron door they'd come through.

Nikki listened closely, but she couldn't hear anything. The knights with all their armor would cause a huge racket in the enclosed tunnel.

"I left orders with Morton, my head butler, to pile crates back on top of the trap door," said the Prince. "And to lock the pantry. He has the only key. He is also the only one in my household besides myself who knows about the trap door and the tunnel. I had the tunnel built thirty years ago, long before any of my current footmen or house-maids came to work for me."

The Prince's face became sober. "Krill has told me of the rumors he heard, that Rufius has tried to bribe some of my servants. I very much hope that none of them gave in to temptation, but there is, of course, no guarantee. I told no one of my plans, except Morton."

"And what exactly are your plans, my lord?" asked Kira.

"To wait in this room until nightfall," said the Prince. "We will not be able to approach the King during the day. He will be in his council chambers surrounded by courtiers, many of whom cannot be trusted. My servants are not the only ones Rufius has tried to bribe. He and Maleficious have handed out many expensive gifts to people who are close to the King." He set Cation down on a table and scratched her under the chin. "After his dinner the King usually retires to his bedchamber unless there is a banquet being held for visiting dignitaries. I am always invited to such gatherings, and as far as I know there is no such event planned for tonight. The castle is large and I learned all its ways and passages in my boyhood. We should be able to travel from this room to the King's bedchamber without being spotted, if we are careful."

The Prince motioned to Krill, who untied a small cloth sack from his belt. Krill set it on a nearby table and pulled out a loaf of brown bread, a large wedge of cheese, and a few apples.

"Not a very elegant repast, I know," said the Prince. "But it should suffice for today. Once the King and I have resolved this business involving Rufius and the Knights of the Iron Fist I will have my cook prepare a feast for you. I'll invite Griff and Posie and the others from your ship."

Nikki took an apple from the table and bit into it thoughtfully. The Prince's remark reminded her strongly of what Athena had said at the imp headquarters – that the King would soon fix all the problems of the Realm. The Prince and Athena were both smart and resourceful people, but Nikki thought they were putting too much faith in the King. He was only one person, no matter how powerful. And judging by everything she'd seen and heard in the last few weeks the King's power was being chipped away by Maleficious and Rufius. Apparently without the King noticing.

She thought back to how lazy the King had seemed when she'd first met him in the gardens of Castle Cogent. That had been her very first day in the Realm, and she' been more than a little shell-shocked by her voyage through the portal to a whole new world. But even so she'd had enough of her wits about her to take stock of the King's personality, and she hadn't really like what she saw. He'd been pleasant and friendly, especially for a monarch everyone in the Realm was supposed to obey, but he'd deferred too much to Maleficious, and even to Athena and Fuzz. He'd been happy to let them run the show if it meant he didn't have to do any work.

The King reminded her of the lab partner she had in AP Chemistry. Suzie Sulminster. How Suzie had gotten into an advanced placement class was a mystery. She spent every class talking on her cell phone and painting her fingernails while Nikki did all the experiments and took all the notes. They hadn't had their big mid-term test yet, but Nikki suspected that Suzie was going to fail it, the same way the King was going to fail to fix all of the Realms problems. Sometimes there was just no substitute for hard work.

Nikki thoughts were interrupted by a loud sneeze from Kira, who had pulled a tarp off a jumbled pile of instruments.

"My lord, what is this?" asked Kira, fanning away a cloud of dust. She pointed at a brass instrument which had a lot of knobs and a little platform with a long brass tube pointed down at it.

Nikki recognized it immediately. It was remarkably similar to the ones she used every day in her biology class. It was a microscope.

"Ah, yes," said the Prince, wiping dust off the instrument with the sleeve of his doublet. "My Grand Magnifier. I built this when I was a lad about Krill's age. Its purpose is to enlarge things, the way a drop of water on a piece of parchment will enlarge the letters underneath it. That was where I got the idea, from the water. I surmised that if water could enlarge something, then possibly glass could as well. Glass ground into different shapes, called lenses. And I was correct."

He removed a small square of glass from the instrument and polished it on his sleeve.

Nikki recognized it as similar to the glass slides they used in her biology class to put specimens on.

The Prince picked one of Cation's hairs off his doublet and placed it on the slide. He put the slide back in the instrument and adjusted several brass knobs. "What the Grand Magnifier does is let you see tiny details which the naked eye cannot see." He waved Kira forward so that she could take a look.

Kira bent her head and looked into the eyepiece the Prince pointed out. She shook her head. "What am I supposed to see, my lord?"

The Prince squinted up at the faint light coming from the grimy round windows and adjusted the instrument again. "The light in here is not good. I doubt these windows have been washed since I was a boy. This instrument works much better if you have an artificial light source. I used to put a stub of candle under the instrument. The light would be caught by this small mirror, illuminating the item you are trying to examine. There are two lenses, one at each end of this brass tube. They enlarge the item. But I dare not light a candle. I fear the light and the smell of the burning wick might attract unwanted attention."

The Prince stroked the instrument as if stroking a beloved pet. "I have a much better Magnifier back in my laboratory which I built only a few years ago, but this little instrument was one of the first things I ever invented." He turned away from it with a sad little smile.

Nikki stepped up to the table and curiously examined the microscope. She squinted into the eyepiece. The Prince was right about the light. The room was too dim to see anything on the specimen slide. But she could tell from the design of the instrument that it was a compound microscope, which meant that it had two lenses. The eyepiece was the top lens and the bottom one near the specimen was called the objective lense. Together the two lenses produced a two-stage magnification which was more powerful that a single lense, such as the one in a magnifying glass. Since technology in the Realm was very basic, Nikki guessed that the lenses in the microscope suffered from what was called the refraction problem. Refraction of light meant that the light was bent as it passed through a lense, causing waviness and blurring the image on the specimen slide. Refraction could also cause the light to break into its component colors, the way a prism split white light into the colors of the rainbow. Refraction was caused by the different speeds which light traveled. It traveled faster through the air than through the glass of a lense. In her world very precise lenses which fixed the refraction problem hadn't been created until the 1850's, when a German engineer named Carl Zeiss started experimenting with optical glass-making techniques. The Realm was a long way away from that type of sophisticated technology.

Nikki turned away from the microscope and sat down on a bench to finish her apple, relieved that in this case she had no conflicting feelings about technology or about trying to balance between two worlds. Nothing would be gained by telling the Prince about how the speed of light was different in different mediums such as air, water, and glass. Back in the hermit camp she'd had no choice but to try to explain to the hermits about epilepsy and seizures, so that she could stop the young hermit from choking on his own vomit during his seizure. She had introduced new knowledge into the Realm in that case, but she'd had to in order to save a life. Here in the Prince's old laboratory there was no life or death situation. She didn't need to bring more ideas from her modern world into the Realm.

Nikki sighed. She was starting to feel like some kind of contagious disease, spreading germs around the unsuspecting Realm. She'd never thought of knowledge as something bad or harmful. Okay, there was the obvious exception of weapons. New knowledge which could be used to create weapons was definitely something she didn't want to spread. Which was why she'd been so horrified when Gwen had shown her that gunpowder experiment back in Deceptionville. The Realm was currently a land free of guns, and that was such a wonderful thing. And the Realm had no explosive devices either. No bombs. Not yet, anyway. Though Gwen had mentioned that the substance she'd invented could be used in mining, to blow away a rock face instead of the current slow method of hacking at the rock with picks and shovels. That was only a small step away from creating a bomb. Not that Gwen would do that, but if her experiment became common knowledge it was only a matter of time before someone would.

Germs. Nikki frowned at the crude little brass microscope on the table. Thinking about spreading new ideas like germs now had her thinking about actual germs. The germ theory of disease hadn't been developed in her world until microscopes became powerful enough to see germs. A dutch scientist working in the late 1600's had been the first to develop a microscope powerful enough to see bacteria in a drop of water. Of course, people hadn't immediately made the connection between disease and the tiny little creatures on the microscope slide, but that had been the start of a huge break-through in medicine which had eventually saved millions of lives. What if, by not telling the Prince all she knew about lenses and the refraction of light, she doomed millions of people in the Realm to die of diseases which might be cured? By knowing about the refraction problem the Prince might be able to perfect his lenses, create a better microscope, see bacteria floating around in a drop of water on his specimen slide, and make the connection between the tiny creatures and a disease like cholera. He could then make sanitation improvements in Kingston and other cities throughout the Realm, preventing cholera, which was caused by sewage getting into drinking water. Nikki had several weeks of personal experience with the Realm's chamber pots and outhouses. Sanitation was practically non-existent. She was willing to bet that many of the wells in the Realm used for drinking water were contaminated with cholera bacteria.

Nikki groaned, putting her head in her hands. One the one hand, by spreading new knowledge in the Realm she could be responsible for getting millions of people killed by new weapons technology. On the other hand, by spreading new knowledge she could be responsible for saving millions of lives through sanitation and disease prevention. It was too much pressure. Her head felt like it was splitting in two.

"Miss, are you all right?" asked Curio, gently patting her on the back. A cloud of dust rose from the tarp which was draped around his shoulders and dragging on the floor.

"I'm okay," said Nikki. "I've just got a headache."

Curio took her by the hand and led her over to a corner where a pile of parchments and tarps had been heaped into a make-shift bed. Kira was stretched out on one end of it, snoring quietly. Curio sat down beside her. "Might as well have a bit of a nap, Miss. Not much else to do til nightfall. It'll make you feel better."

Nikki nodded and curled up beside him. Cation padded over and kneaded Nikki's back until it was the right consistency for snuggling up to. Nikki dozed off to the sound of Cation's purring.

Chapter Eight

✦

And the Walls Fell Down

NIKKI WAS TOTALLY lost. They'd been following the Prince along what seemed like miles of passageways. The Southern Castle had to be the biggest castle ever built. Hundreds of rooms, dozens of winding staircases, endless stone passages. Fortunately the area they were in seemed to be mostly abandoned. Occasionally they heard the footsteps of armor-clad guards, but the guards made so much noise that they had plenty of time to hide.

"In here," whispered the Prince after a long climb up a winding stone staircase. He herded them into a small room which had a white marble fireplace and a patterned carpet on the parquet floor.

They had to be getting close to the King's chamber, thought Nikki. This was the fanciest room they'd hid in so far.

"I'll be back in a moment," whispered the Prince. "The King doesn't usually keep a guard on his chambers, but that may have changed. If I'm not back in an hour, make your way back to my old laboratory. If I am not able to come there myself I'll send word to Morton, my head butler. He'll help you in any way he can."

The Prince left, quietly shutting the door behind him. Nikki was pretty sure the others were thinking the same thing she was. Getting back to the Prince's laboratory was next to impossible. The castle was so huge, with such a rabbit-warren of passages, that none of them had the slightest idea where they were or how to re-trace their steps. She walked over to the leaded-pane window and looked out. The moon was shining on the castle's battlements. The room they were in was very high up, with a long drop to a courtyard filled with what looked like orange and lemon trees. A fountain spouted a jet of water into the moonlight. Nikki could just make out the tiny figures of armed guards patrolling the courtyard. The Southern Castle was a strange mix of beauty and weaponry, Nikki thought. Castle Cogent, the King's main residence, was not nearly so warlike. She guessed that most of the armed guards here had been put in place by Maleficious. She wondered if Maleficious and Rufius were setting the Southern Castle up as a kind of military power base. A rival to Castle Cogent. A power split like that could easily lead to civil war. Nikki shuddered. The thought of getting caught in a war horrified her. Her first instinct was to get back to the portal near Castle Cogent as fast as she could. To return to her own world. Her failure at the Wisconsin state debate championship and her petty little problems with Tina, the captain of the debate team, seemed wildly unimportant now. But she knew she couldn't go home yet, and not just because the portal was so far away. She had made friends here in the Realm. Athena, Fuzz, Gwen, Curio, Kira. Even Krill and the Prince. She didn't want to see any of them hurt, not if she could help it. Though exactly what she could do to prevent a war, well, she had no idea. But she couldn't just run away.

The door suddenly creaked open and all of them jumped, but it was just the Prince.

He beckoned to them. "Hurry. There is no guard in front of the King's chambers, but there is a patrol. It has just gone past. We need to get inside before they return."

They followed him on tiptoe up a short flight of marble stairs. The balusters were carved into the shapes of imps holding bouquets of roses. The workmanship of the carvings was exquisite, but Nikki thought the marble imps looked silly and simpering. Athena and Fuzz never looked like that. Athena always looked stern and unbending, and Fuzz usually looked sarcastic. She could imagine Fuzz rolling his eyes at the marble imps every time he climbed this staircase.

At the top was a landing covered with a lush purple carpet. Torches in brackets shone on a sparkling mosaic of gold and enamel which covered the walls. It depicted the castle, Kingston, and the ships in the harbor. Nikki even spotted a tiny gold version of the Prince's mansion.

The Prince knocked on a heavy brass door at the end of the landing. It swung silently open and they all filed inside. The person who had opened the door closed it after them and locked it with a key as big as Nikki's hand.

"Fuzz!" gasped Nikki.

Fuzz checked that the door was firmly locked and gave her a wicked grin. "It's about time. Took you forever to get here. I got to Kingston a week ago. Of course, you'd have gotten here sooner if Athena hadn't lost you."

"Lost them! Fuzz, you woolly-brained good-for-nothing dunderhead, I didn't . . ."

Athena's protests were muffled as Nikki rushed forward and knelt down, hugging the little imp tightly.

Athena patted her. "There, there, Miss. No point in crying. Everyone is safe and sound." The imp gently pushed Nikki away and smoothed her gray dress. She pulled a folded white handkerchief out of her sleeve and loudly blew her nose. "No point in crying at all. It is a total waste of time."

"If you're done not crying we should take them to the King," said Fuzz.

"Of course, of course," said Athena, giving her eyes a last swipe with the handkerchief and tucking it back in her sleeve. She gave Curio a quick smile and a pat on the arm and shook hands with the Prince. "Good to see you again, my lord," she said.

"The pleasure is always mine, dear Athena," said the Prince.

Athena glanced up at Kira and way up at Krill. "I don't believe I know these two young people."

Kira bent down and politely shook hands with the imp. "I am called Kira, ma'am. And this is my brother Krill. We are sailors on the vessel called the Sunfish. Griff, a relative of the Prince, is our captain. We were anchored about a day's sail up the coast from Kingston when we happened across these two." She waved her hand at Nikki and Curio. "Half starved, they were, from a long journey through the Trackless Forest. We fed them and took them aboard the Sunfish."

Athena sniffled and the handkerchief made another appearance. "Half starved, you say? Oh, my dears. To think that you have been in such difficulties. And it was all my fault. I . . ." She buried her face in the handkerchief.

"Nonsense," said Nikki, giving the imp another hug and gently pulling the handkerchief away from her face. She wiped Athena's tears and firmly tucked the handkerchief back into its hiding place. "It wasn't in any way your fault."

"Well . . ." began Fuzz, but he lapsed into silence when Nikki shot him a warning look.

"Not your fault at all, Miss," piped up Curio. "It was my fault if it was anyone's. I panicked, back at the hermit camp. I was afraid they were going to hurt Miss Nikki, so after I got her out of the hut I ran into the forest. She had no choice but to follow me. It was tough going, but we followed the Bunny and came out right in the end."

"How did you get here so fast?" Nikki asked Fuzz. "Athena said it would take you much longer, since you had to go around the Trackless Forest."

Fuzz laughed. "We hitched a ride with those armor-plated doofuses, those Knights of the Iron Fist. Gwen and I were tramping along the Great Southern Road toward the coast when we heard a huge racket on the road behind us. We hid in the bushes and watched as a long column of knights on horseback rode past. They were going in the direction we wanted to go, so we just snuck aboard one of their supply wagons. Hid behind some barrels of ale. Those knights don't stint themselves, that's for sure. That ale was top quality Amber Foam, straight from the Beadle Brewery in the Haunted Hills. The Haunted Hills aren't good for much, but they do brew some great ale. I'll give them that."

Nikki looked around the small anteroom they were in. "So, where's Gwen?" she asked. "Is she in the castle?"

Fuzz looked troubled and glanced sideways at Athena.

"Miss Gwendolyn is being housed in a different part of the castle," said Athena, avoiding Nikki's eye.

Nikki frowned down at her. "What does that mean? Can we go see her?"

Athena shook her head sadly. "No, Miss. I have tried, but Miss Gwendolyn is not allowed visitors."

Nikki's eyes flashed angrily. "Not allowed visitors! That sounds like she's in jail or something."

Athena shook her head vigorously. "No, Miss. Not at all. The King himself arranged for Miss Gwendolyn to be housed in a very comfortable suite of rooms used for foreign dignitaries. The Head Chamberlain showed me those rooms once, many years ago when I was visiting Kingston. They are very nice, with rich furnishings and their own little courtyard with a fountain in the middle. Miss Gwendolyn is very comfortable."

Nikki folded her arms. "I don't care whether she's comfortable or not, I want to know why I can't visit her. I . . ."

She stopped speaking as the inner door of the anteroom suddenly swung open. The King walked in. He wasn't wearing his crown, but otherwise he looked appropriately regal in a black doublet embroidered with gold thread.

He walked straight up to Nikki and shook her hand. "So you've arrived at last. Wonderful, wonderful. All my emissaries are together again. Athena was getting a bit worried, you know. I told her everything would work out just fine, and it has. Worrying solves nothing. That's my motto. Things will work out if you just leave them alone."

He turned to the Prince and clapped him on the shoulder. "Ambrose! Good to see you again. It's been too long. I was just about to have a late supper. You and your friends will join me, of course."

The King disappeared back through the inner door without waiting for an answer.

The Prince smiled ruefully. He shrugged and motioned for them to follow the King.

The room they entered was not nearly as grand as Nikki had been expecting. She'd imagined a fancier version of the Prince's dining room, but this room looked like it could use a bit of housecleaning. Cushions were falling off chairs, and a pair of boots and a purple velvet cloak had been left on the floor. The large oak dining table in the middle of the room was polished to a high gloss, but manuscripts were scattered along one end of it and an overturned ink pot dripped ink onto the parquet floor.

The King chuckled and righted the ink pot. "Sorry about the mess. Maleficious has spent all day informing me on the state of the Realm, and he seemed to think that his presentation was for my ears only. His secretiveness can be quite annoying at times. He wouldn't even let any of the servants in here to clean. Don't tell the old boy I said so, but he can be quite the windbag. I finally had to plead hunger to get him to wrap it up. He departed for his own quarters not half an hour ago."

The Prince looked at him sharply, the dark scar on his cheek twitching. "So, Maleficious is residing here permanently, is he?"

The King shrugged, taking his place at the head of the table and motioning the rest of them to join him. "Well, he has to live some-where, doesn't he old chap? He has quarters here and at Castle Cogent. Just now he's quite busy here in Kingston, developing trade between the Realm and the Southern Isles. He tells me the trade should generate a nice bump in tax income. Which the Realm could use, quite frankly. I don't know where the money goes sometimes. It seems to pour out of my treasury like water."

"More like wine into the goblets of Maleficious and Rufius," muttered Fuzz under his breath. He jumped and rubbed his shin where Athena had kicked him under the table.

"Maleficious has done his best to manage the accounts," contin-ued the King, removing a linen napkin from a silver dish of buttered rolls and passing it to Athena. "But numbers aren't really his strong suit. More of a high-level thinker, is Maleficious. His apprentice, that young man called Rufius, now there's someone who understands finances. He's been indispensable in managing the treasury. Between the two of them they've got the income and the expenses and the taxes down to a fine art. I hardly need to glance at a ledger these days. They take care of it all. Quite a load off my mind, to be honest. I'm even worse than Maleficious at figures. When I was a lad my tutor nearly tore his hair out trying to teach me sums." He chuckled and passed a platter of roast beef to the Prince, who was sitting on his right.

The Prince speared a piece of beef, frowning down at it as if it had personally offended him. "Do you think it wise, my lord, to give up so many of your duties to Maleficious and his underlings? It is, after all, your kingdom, not his."

The King slapped him on the back. "Ambrose, if it were up to you you'd have me working myself to death. You forget that I don't have your fanatical industriousness. You slave night and day in that laboratory of yours, barely coming up for air. I don't know how you do it. It seems a joyless existence." He shook his head and turned to

Athena on his left. "So, do you think there will be room for your companions in your quarters? It seems to me you will all be terribly cramped. I'm glad to see you, but I fail to see why you insist on being stuck in here with me. There are any number of grand suites in the castle I could have readied for you and your guests."

He turned to the others. "Fuzz and Athena have been staying in one of the small guest rooms here in my very modest quarters in the Lookout Tower. The views up here are spectacular, the best in the city, which is why I always stay here when I'm in Kingston. I used to come up here as a boy, to gaze out at the sea. But the quarters are not spacious."

"We will manage, my lord," said Athena. "We have things to discuss, and I'd rather not have our friends scattered all over the castle."

The King smiled. "And of course you don't want Maleficious to find out you're here." He poured wine into a silver goblet. "My advisors have had a bit of a falling out, I'm afraid. Fuzz and Athena have never gotten along with Maleficious, and lately they have been avoiding him entirely." He shook his head like an affectionate parent saddened by his children fighting.

Nikki breathed a sigh of relief. So Fuzz and Athena were safe, at least for now. No one except the King knew they were here. She smiled at the irony. Maleficious and Rufius had been searching all over the Realm for the imps, and here they were right in the King's quarters. And it seemed that they were all safe from the Knights of the Iron Fist. Even if the Knights found the trap door in the Prince's mansion and followed the tunnel to his old laboratory in the castle they wouldn't dare to enter the King's quarters. The King was still the leader of the Realm, though even an outsider like herself could see that the King's power was cracking. Maleficious, Rufius, and the Knights seemed on the verge of attempting a coup.

The King drank another goblet of wine and began a long tale of his boyhood adventures in Kingston. The Prince sat through this story impatiently tapping his fingers and frowning down at the table. Finally he cut in as the King was relating how he'd fallen into Kingston harbor and been rescued by a fisherman. "My lord, this is all very amusing, but we have something important to discuss. I am afraid it cannot wait."

The King set his goblet down and politely turned to the Prince. "Of course, Ambrose. I am all ears."

"My lord, you may not be aware of this, but there are armed knights surrounding my house as we speak."

The King's mouth dropped open. "Armed knights? Are you referring to the Knight of the Iron Fist?"

The Prince nodded, his thin mouth tightening.

"Well, that explains it," said the King, laughing and sitting back in his chair.

Everyone looked at him in confusion, unsure how this explained anything at all.

"My dear chap, no one is surrounding your house. The knights are in town for a tournament. You know, jousting, archery, sword play, that sort of thing. It was Maleficious's idea. He felt it would be good for the local economy. There are participants coming to Kingston from all up and down the south coast. Should be heaps of fun. I'll be handing out the prizes myself. If the knights alarmed you or your servants my apologies, but they were just paying you a visit as one of Kingston's most important citizens."

Nikki watched the Prince study the King. She could tell the Prince was baffled as to how to proceed, probably not a thing which happened to him very often. The Prince knew very well that the knights' visit had not been a social call, but trying to convince the King of that was going to be difficult. Especially since she suspected that the King didn't *want* to be convinced of that.

"My lord," the Prince finally said, "these knights rode their horses through my gardens and right up to my front door. They were fully armed with spear and sword, and they demanded that I turn one of my guests over to them. These are not the actions of men paying a polite visit."

The King waved a hand dismissively. "Ambrose, you judge them too harshly. You are a scholar, not a fighting man. You don't understand the rough ways of these knights. They were undoubtedly just playing a prank on you. A practical joke. One in bad taste, by the sound of it, but still harmless."

The Prince sighed and ran a hand through his hair, leaving it standing on end. He was just about to speak when all of a sudden a huge boom shook the tower. Bits of plaster fell from the ceiling and the platter of roast beef skittered off the table and crashed to the floor.

They all jumped up, dropping their knives and forks and knocking their chairs over.

The only person still sitting was the King, who was trembling in his chair, his face white. "What on earth? Ambrose, what was that?"

The Prince shook his head. "I don't know, my lord." He strode to one of the narrow windows of the tower and peered out. "There is some kind of damage to the castle. Not to this tower, but to a section nearby. On the lowest level."

The rest of them rushed to the windows.

Nikki squinted into the darkness where the Prince was pointing. The castle walls were not well lit, but there were a few scattered torches in wall-brackets on the lower levels. She could just make out a pile of rubble against one of the buttresses. Dust was drifting up from it. It looked like a hole had been blown in one of the castle walls. She opened the leaded-glass window to get a better look. As the fresh night air wafted in Nikki knew immediately what had caused the loud boom. She recognized the smell at once. She had smelled the same thing in chemistry class, when her teacher had demonstrated the effect of combining sulfur, charcoal, and potassium nitrate. Gunpowder.

Gwen. *That* was why Gwen was housed in a different part of the castle, and not allowed visitors. Nikki would bet her entire allowance for a year that Rufius was behind this. He must have learned of Gwen's experiment with gunpowder from that Lurker they'd seen watching them in Deceptionville. He had locked her up here in the castle and ordered her to make gunpowder for him. Though, how Rufius had managed to capture Gwen without finding out about Fuzz and Athena being in the castle was a mystery. Maybe Fuzz and Gwen had gotten separated on the rode to Kingston.

"Look!" said Kira. "Someone is climbing out of that hole in the wall."

Nikki gasped. Even in the weak light from the torches Gwen's pale blond hair shone like a beacon. They watched as the small figure stumbled down the pile of rubble and disappeared into a dark courtyard. They could hear cries of alarm, and see the figures of several guards leaning over a parapet, but no one followed Gwen out of the hole.

Nikki leaned against the windowsill, her knees shaking. It seemed Gwen had escaped. She had blown up the wall of her prison. But where would she go? She was far from her home in Deceptionville, and even farther from her mother's house, Muddled Manor. Nikki glanced worriedly over at Athena. The imp was staring at her intently.

Athena came over to her and took Nikki's hand. "We will find her, Miss. I promise. No harm will come to Miss Gwendolyn."

Nikki smiled down at the imp, trying to look reassured. She and Gwen were both a long way from home. And she wasn't sure if either of them would ever get back.

End of Book Two

Nikki's adventures in the Realm of Reason continue in the third book
of the *Logic to the Rescue* series: *The Bard of Biology*.

The Logic to the Rescue series

Logic to the Rescue
The Prince of Physics
The Bard of Biology
Mystics and Medicine
The Sorcerer of the Stars

The Hamsters Rule series

Hamsters Rule, Gerbils Drool
Hamsters Rule the School

Excerpt from The Bard of Biology

Chapter One

—◆◆—

The Tournament

NIKKI SWORE AS her mask slipped over her eyes. She stopped to adjust it. Little ten-year-old Curio, who was walking behind her, bumped into her.

"Sorry, Miss," said Curio, backing up into a row of rustling corn stalks. "It must be a bother having to wear that."

Nikki blinked as bright sunlight streamed into her mask's eyeholes again. "It's more than a bother. It's hot and itchy and it keeps slipping over my eyes. You're lucky you don't have to wear this getup."

She waved her hands vaguely over herself from head to foot. She was wearing not only a mask but also a hooded cloak and a floor-length robe, all made of rough white linen. It was the style of clothing worn by a local cult called the Seekers. The Seekers believed that sunlight on the skin poisoned the mind, or some such nonsense. Nikki hadn't really paid much attention to the Prince's description of the cult. Its members were apparently a common sight in the city of Kingston, so the Prince had decided their style of dress would be an ideal disguise for Nikki. The palace guards were searching for her everywhere, so hiding her face was the only way she could move about freely in public.

Nikki swore again as she tripped over her robe. In their hasty flight from the Southern Castle there'd been no time to adjust the robe's length. She held it up with one hand while holding her mask with the other. Her rucksack was strapped to her back under the hooded cloak and she could feel the rucksack squirming. Not to mention growling. Cation was not happy. She felt a tiny paw swat at her neck. Reaching awkwardly under the cloak she nudged the kitten back down into the depths of the rucksack. "Where exactly are we going?" she asked Athena, who was stumbling along a ploughed furrow in the corn field a few feet ahead. The imp was also dressed as a Seeker, and her short stature made her look like a young child converted to the cult.

"We are headed for the King's tournament, Miss," said Athena. "Most of the people in Kingston will be headed there today. It is a very special event and is very popular. By noontime there will be few people left in the city. Everyone will be out at the fairgrounds. It is the Prince's opinion that Miss Gwendolyn will head for the tournament also, once she notices how empty the city is becoming. It will be safer for her to stay with the crowds."

"I guess that's as good a plan as any," said Nikki.

"Will you two keep it down?" hissed Fuzz, who was leading the way. He was having less trouble walking than the others, as his robe and cloak were a bit too short for him. His dusty leather boots and woolen trousers could be seen beneath the hem of the cloak. "There could be palace guards all over this corn field."

Athena sniffed. "That is highly doubtful. If those ridiculous guards with all their clumsy armor were trampling through the corn they would be making a noise like stampeding buffalo."

"Yeah, well, keep it down anyway," grumbled Fuzz. "You two don't sound anything like typical Seekers. I've met a few on my visits to Kingston, and believe me, they are just about the dumbest people in the Realm. They can barely string two words together. All they do is mumble about things they call spirit beings and how these beings are always whispering stuff into their ears. You wouldn't believe how many of them drown each year. They wander around, listening to the voices in their heads, and walk straight off the Kingston cliffs. The local fishermen find one of them tangled in their herring nets every few months. It's enough to make you swear off fish dinners."

Athena impatiently waved him to silence. They had reached the edge of the corn field. In front of them stretched a wide open area of grassy pastureland. A herd of cows clustered near the corn stalks, nervously eyeing a long row of canvas tents which had invaded their pasture. Hundreds of people were milling around the tents, with more pouring into the field every second. Most of the tents had trestle tables set up in front with things for sale. The baker and brewer tents had the longest lines. People jostled to buy just-baked pastries and foaming tankards of ale. In one corner of the field children were flying kites made of royal blue and crimson silk. The kites swooped and dived like giant birds. Just beyond the kites in a large area of trampled grass men were wrestling and fighting with clanking swords. Each fighter was surrounded by a crowd of gamblers waving money and shouting loudly at their chosen contestants.

"We will separate," whispered Athena. Fuzz immediately started to protest but she dismissed him with a wave of her hand. "It is not ideal, but we will search much faster that way. We all know what Miss Gwendolyn looks like, but remember, she may be in disguise. The palace guards are undoubtedly searching for her." She pointed to four different sections of the pasture. "I will take the area over by the kites. Fuzz, you take the wrestlers. Curio, you take that area bordering the woods, and Miss, you take the area where the tents are. We will meet back here in the cornfield in two hours."

Nikki automatically looked down at her wrist, where the faint tan-line from her watch was still visible. She hadn't been wearing it when

Fuzz and Athena brought her through the portal at her high school. She'd never seen a watch in the Realm of Reason. There'd been a sundial in Deceptionville, but that was the only kind of time-keeping device she'd ever seen in the Realm. "How will we know when two hours are up?" she whispered.

Athena pointed back toward Kingston, where the towers of the Southern Castle loomed dark against the morning sun. "It is about eight o'clock now, Miss. Watch the sun. When it is just above the tallest tower in the castle it will be ten o'clock."

Nikki nodded and reluctantly stepped out from the cover of the corn stalks. She watched as the other three disappeared into the crowd. She was temporarily alone in the Realm of Reason again and the familiar feeling of anxiety crept over her. She hitched up her robe and tried to focus on her mission. Find Gwen.

As she stumbled across the rutted grass of the pasture her first thought was to look for someone dressed as a Seeker. It was a handy disguise and there were several of the hooded figures about. She eyed them as they passed, but none seemed to match Gwen's height or slender build. Also, just like Fuzz had said, they were all mumbling to themselves. She could imagine Gwen using the Seeker robes as a disguise, but it seemed unlikely that she'd try to copy their mumbling. It was a bright sunny day and most of the tournament-goers were not wearing hoods or cloaks. Gwen couldn't just throw a hood over her pale blond hair, not without people wondering why she was over-dressed for the hot weather. Maybe she'd found a way to dye her hair? As Nikki mulled this over her attention was caught by gasps coming from a tent nearby. She edged through the throng.

A wooden table set up in front of the tent held a collection of objects which immediately reminded her of her freshman physics class. On top of a blue velvet cloth lay two glass rods about a foot in length. Next to the rods was a wooden structure about a foot tall, with a string hanging from it. An elderly man dressed in a shiny gold robe picked up one of the glass rods. He waved it dramatically over his head then rubbed it vigorously with a piece of silk. He tied the glass rod onto the piece of string so that it swung freely in the air. Then he rubbed the other glass rod with the silk. He held the second rod close to the first one, careful not to let them touch. The crowd gasped as the glass rod on the string swung away from the other rod as if pushed by invisible hands.

The electrostatic force, thought Nikki. She'd done this very same experiment in her physics class. When the glass rod was rubbed with silk some of the rod's electrons were transferred to the piece of silk. Since electrons were negative, losing some of them left the glass rod with a positive charge. Since the other glass rod also had a positive charge the two rods repelled each other, causing them to move away from each other as if by magic. The technical term for it was electrostatic repulsion. Same charges repelled, opposite charges attracted.

A small boy clutched the edge of the table, hopping up and down excitedly. "What's making it move? Huh? What's making it?"

The man standing next to him smiled and put a restraining hand on the boy's head. "Careful now, son. You'll scare 'em away."

"Scare who away, Pa? Who? Who?"

"The sprites, of course," said the man. "Them as what's making the rods move." He pulled a coin out of his trouser pocket and tossed it into a little box on the table.

The elderly man in the gold robe made him a formal little bow. He scooped up the coin in his liver-spotted hand and tucked it into a pouch at his waist.

"Sprites, Father? But how cum I can't see 'em? Can you see 'em? Do they have wings? How do you know they're there? Huh? How?"

The boy poked a curious finger into the space between the two rods, but withdrew it hastily when the old man glared at him.

"I know them sprites are there cuz the rods are moving, ain't they?" said the boy's father. "Don't be wasting time with daft questions."

The man led his son away and Nikki stared thoughtfully after them. It was strange, she thought. When people in the Realm of Reason didn't understand something they had the same tendency to invent invisible beings as people in her own world did. Though people in her own world had started to move past that kind of thinking about three-hundred years ago, with the start of the scientific revolution. They had started to examine nature more honestly and rigorously, instead of just making up wild stories about magic and invisible spirits. The Realm of Reason, on the other hand, seemed to be stuck firmly in the invisible-being stage. She wondered if it would ever start to move away from that kind of superstition. It was a long and difficult process, and it seemed to require a few brave and inventive people to kick it off. In her world it had been people like Galileo, Newton, and Leonardo da Vinci, who had been not only an artist but also an engineer and naturalist, famous for his anatomically accurate drawings of people, animals, and insects. Here in the Realm of Reason some of its citizens had begun to take small steps down that path. Gwen, for one, and the Prince of Physics, for another. Athena and Curio also seemed headed in that direction, though they didn't do experiments the way Gwen and the Prince did. They were just open-minded and curious, and willing to evaluate evidence. Even Kira, an uneducated sailor, had started down the path of reason due to her expertise in navigation. Perhaps there was hope for the Realm yet.

"Hey! You. Yes, I'm talking to you, Missy."

Nikki jumped. The old man in the gold robe was waving his finger menacingly in her direction.

"You just take yourself off, now," he said. "Don't want your kind hanging around. Never get so much as a single coin from you nutters, do I? You just move along and make room for paying customers."

Nikki hitched up her Seeker's robe and disappeared back into the crowd. The last thing she wanted was to cause a scene and have the palace guards show up to see what the commotion was. She had spotted some of the guards on the outskirts of the pasture, quietly watching the crowd. She was surprised that they hadn't been combing the tournament looking for Gwen, which made her nervous. Did Rufius have other, less conspicuous people out looking for her? The palace guards, with their shiny, clunking armor, were easy to spot and easy to avoid. But if Rufius had searchers dressed as ordinary citizens of Kingston that made things a lot more difficult. That smiling lady carrying a tray of pastries could be one of his searchers, or that man drinking a tankard of ale with such gusto that half of it was spilling down his tunic. Nikki raised an eyebrow as the man suddenly dropped his tankard and fell face first into the grass. Okay, maybe not him, she thought.

She weaved carefully through the crowd, trying to stay as inconspicuous as possible. She passed by the long lines at the brewers tents without giving the customers a second glance. It was unlikely that Gwen would stop to drink a tankard of ale while trying to flee from Rufius and his guards. She noticed that the crowd was starting to thin out. People were leaving the tent area and heading to the trampled grass where the wrestling and sword fighting was taking place. A burst of trumpet calls sounded and banners with pictures of swords and arrows were raised. It looked like some sort of competition was about to begin.

Nikki ducked under a canvas awning to get out of the flow of foot traffic. Under the shade of the awning was a stall selling potted plants of all sorts – parsley, basil, thyme, petunias, tomatoes, zucchini, string beans, marigolds, and lots of other plants she didn't recognize.

"Gotta rush, dearie," said a customer, handing a coin to the stall's owner. "The tourney's about to begin. I put a pile o'coin on Kincaid's son to take the medal in the broadsword. He's a big, strapping lad and swings that sword around like an angry bear. If he doesn't trip over his own feet he should do well." She hurried away with a potted begonia under her arm.

"Not going to the tournament?" asked a quiet voice.

Nikki jumped. The other customers had left and the owner of the stall was looking at her. The woman was about fifty, Nikki judged, with long brown hair turning gray and kind brown eyes. She wore a long woolen dress splotched with dirt from her potted plants and her fingernails were blackened with soil.

Nikki's first instinct was to dart away. If she spoke the woman would probably notice that she wasn't a real Seeker. She considered trying to fake a Seeker mumble, but the woman was looking at her so kindly that Nikki found herself smiling under her mask. "I don't find wrestling or sword-fighting all that interesting," she said.

The woman smiled, the laugh lines around her eyes crinkling. "Nor do I. All that bashing and grunting. Quite uncivilized." She held out a ripe peach. "Have one. No charge. The trees in my orchard produced so many this year that they're rotting on the branches."

Nikki took the plump, fuzzy fruit. "Thanks. That's very nice of you." She raised her face mask up just enough to slip the peach under it and took a bite. "Mmm. Wonderful." As she chewed she noticed that the woman was petting something in her hand. It was a tiny, pure-white mouse, no longer than one of the woman's fingers. As she watched it ran up the woman's arm and perched on top of her head.

The woman laughed and plucked the mouse off of her head. "This is Rosie. I raised her from a pup, when she was no bigger than my fingernail. Rosie is a nickname, of course. Her full name is Rosamund, and her title is the Rose of Knowledge."

Rosie let out a squeak, as if acknowledging that it was obvious a mouse of her distinction would have a title.

Nikki laughed. "Can I hold her?"

The woman nodded and gently placed Rosie in Nikki's palm.

Nikki stroked the mouse's soft fur. Rosie peered up at her with sharp black eyes and her tiny nose twitched, as if she'd seen through

Nikki's Seeker mask and knew she was an imposter. Nikki felt Cation squirm inside her rucksack and she quickly handed the mouse back to the woman.

"I'm Linnea, by the way," said the woman.

"Oh, like the Linnaean System," said Nikki without thinking.

The woman's eyebrows rose in surprise. "The what?"

Nikki mentally smacked herself on the head. Seekers from the Realm of Reason didn't go around making remarks about a system of classifying species. Especially since the Linnaean System hadn't been invented in the Realm but in her own world by a Swedish botanist called Carl Linnaeus. The system organized all plants and animals into a hierarchy of kingdom, class order, genus, and species. Linnaeus had developed his system nearly three hundred years ago, and the modern system had added family and phylum to the system, though she could never remember where they went. Was it phylum, kingdom, class? Or kingdom, phylum, class? She'd failed that exact question about the Linnaean System on her Biology mid-term. "Um, nothing," mumbled Nikki. "It's not important."

The woman was still looking at her curiously. She pointed at Nikki's hands. "You don't wear gloves," she said. "Kind of unusual, isn't it? All the Seekers I've ever seen have worn long gloves, all the way up to their elbows. They're terrified of any sunlight hitting their skin."

"Um . . ." said Nikki, pulling her hands inside the long sleeves of her robe. As she tried to think up some excuse for her bare hands she suddenly noticed that Linnea was looking past her with a tense expression on her face. Nikki turned and found herself face to face with Rufius.

He was dressed in his usual spotless black tunic. This one had silver filigree around the neckline and along the hem. His sandals were so clean that he could have been walking through a palace rather than a muddy cow pasture. His black eyes slid over Nikki's mask, robe, and cloak.

Nikki stood still as stone. A bead of sweat trickled down her neck. In the rucksack on her back she could feel Cation squirming. Did Seekers have pets? If a meow came from under her cloak would it be a dead giveaway that she was an impostor?

Linnea's voice interrupted Nikki's panicked thoughts. "She's just a Seeker, my lord. She wanted some fruit to take back to the other members of her order." She gestured impatiently at Nikki. "In the back, girl. Inside the tent. I set aside a basket of apples for you. You can pay me later."

Nikki felt Rufius watching her as she passed through the rows of potted plants and into the cool darkness of the heavy canvas tent. Baskets and boxes piled high with peaches, apples, and pears filled the tent. The air was heavy with the scent of ripe fruit and potting soil. In the back of the tent loomed a row of potted fruit trees. Nikki ducked behind these and peered out from between the branches. Linnea was pointing off into the distance toward the sword-fighting area of the pasture. Rufius glanced briefly in the direction she was pointing, then turned back and stared at the tent.

"He's going to come in!" whispered a voice right behind Nikki.

Nikki gasped and nearly fell face-first into the potted trees.

"Shhh! He'll hear you!"

It was Gwendolyn, hiding behind a potted blueberry bush. Her face was smudged with soot, her grey dress had a large burn mark on the skirt, and one of her hands was wrapped in a bloody bandage.

Nikki crawled behind the blueberry bush and gave Gwen a quick hug. "It's so good to see you again. Are you hurt?" she whispered.

Gwendolyn didn't answer. She was staring intently out at Rufius.

Linnea was now standing in front of him, blocking the way into the tent. Rosie the mouse was perched on her head, squeaking furiously at Rufius.

Nikki gasped. Rufius had raised his hand, and it looked for a moment like he was going to hit Linnea. But instead he raised his fingers to his lips and gave a piercing whistle. Somewhere out in the pasture a clanking sound began, drawing closer and closer to the tent.

"Guards!" whispered Gwendolyn. "Come on!" She grabbed Nikki's sleeve and pulled her toward the back of the tent. The canvas sides of the tent were held down by wooden spikes driven into the ground. Gwendolyn snatched up a trowel from a box of gardening tools and attacked the dirt around a spike. When the spike was loose she grabbed it and pulled. A six-inch gap appeared, just high enough for them to squirm under. Gwendolyn was through in a flash, but the gap wasn't high enough for both Nikki and her rucksack. She wriggled in frustration, trapped by her heavy Seeker robes. Cation yowled from inside the rucksack.

"Come on!" hissed Gwendolyn, pulling on Nikki's shoulders.

"Guards! In here!" shouted a voice only a few feet away. Rufius was right behind them, inside the tent.

Nikki gave one last desperate squirm and Gwendolyn yanked with all her might. Darkness suddenly descended on them. The tent had collapsed. Behind her she heard Rufius swearing. Nikki crawled in the opposite direction, pushing through the heavy canvas folds of the collapsed tent. She felt a tug on her arm and Gwendolyn pulled her out onto the grass behind the tent.

Nikki ripped off her face mask and squirmed out of her heavy Seeker cloak and robe. Underneath she wore her jeans and the blue silk tunic which Kira had given her back at the Prince's house. Much better. Now she could run. The only question was which way. She glanced quickly over her shoulder. The lump which was Rufius was still wrestling with the collapsed tent. She could hear the palace guards approaching but none were in sight yet.

"Now what?" she whispered to Gwen. "I was supposed to meet Athena, Fuzz, and Curio at the corn field on the outskirts of the pasture."

Gwen shook her head. "We don't want to lead Rufius and his guards straight to them. Follow me."

Chapter Two

The Rose of Knowledge

NIKKI STRETCHED OUT full length on the lawn, wriggling her bare feet in delight. After hours of running through the countryside around Kingston, hiding from every passerby, it was sheer heaven to lay still and rest. She closed her eyes as a cool breeze wafted the smell of ripening peaches over her. She hadn't explored all of it yet, but Linnea's garden was quickly becoming her favorite place in the Realm of Reason.

Linnea's thatched-roof house was tucked away deep in a valley miles from Kingston. It was surrounded by flower gardens, rows of vegetables, wide green lawns and orchards of fruit trees. According to Gwen they would be spending several days here while they tried to track down Athena, Fuzz, and Curio. That was fine with Nikki. She needed a bit of a vacation from her adventures. It had been a whirlwind of activity ever since she stepped through that old boiler in the janitor's closet back home. She just hoped that Linnea was right about this place being impossible for Rufius and his guards to find. She wasn't sure exactly what Rufius would do if he caught her and Gwen, but she had a feeling that a dungeon was involved and she'd seen enough of the one in Castle Cogent to last a lifetime. Rats, cockroaches and the smell of raw sewage were not her favorite things.

"These strange shoes are falling apart. We'll have to see about getting you some new ones."

Nikki opened one eye. Gwen was holding up one of her Nikes. The rubber sole had almost completely detached from the uppers. Running all over the countryside had torn them up beyond repair.

Gwen prodded the sole with her finger. "What is this material?" she asked.

"Rubber," said Nikki. "Artificial rubber, anyway."

Gwen folded and twisted the sole. "It's so malleable. We don't have anything like it here in the Realm. How is it made?"

"Originally it came from rubber trees," said Nikki. "From the sap of the rubber tree. They used to carve a shallow trough into the bark of the tree. The sap would run down the trough and collect in a bucket. But I don't think my shoes are made of real rubber. My land produces an artificial kind of rubber." She closed her eyes again and hoped that Gwen was going to drop the subject. Trying to explain about artificial rubber was going to involve details about her world she wasn't sure she wanted to get into. She'd never really discussed her world with Gwen. Gwen knew she was a foreigner, but she didn't know from where. Athena and Fuzz had warned her not to let people know that she wasn't from the Realm of Reason. She'd tried to follow their advice, but it was hard with people she liked, like Gwen, Curio, and Kira. It was natural to want to share stuff about your life with friends, and Gwen was the closest thing to a friend she had in the Realm. She was fond of Athena and Fuzz, but they were a lot older than she was, and they had important things to do. Like trying to prevent Rufius and Maleficious from taking over the Realm.

As far as she knew, Athena, Fuzz, and the King were the only people in the Realm who knew where she came from. She thought back to her first meeting with Gwen at Gwen's ancestral home, Muddled Manor. She'd been so thrilled to meet someone who loved chemistry as much as she did that she'd told Gwen a lot about her high school's chemistry lab and the technical equipment it had. She'd just arrived in the Realm and hadn't had time to understand just how backward the Realm was in terms of scientific discoveries. And it was only after she'd met greedy and ruthless people in the Realm, people like Rufius, Fortuna, and Avaricious, people who might use technology to harm others, that she'd realized she needed to be careful about what she said.

"This artificial rubber . . ." began Gwen.

"There you two are."

Nikki tilted her head back and squinted up at the sloping lawn. Linnea was coming toward them with Rosie the mouse riding proudly on top of her head like a tiny white figurehead on a sailing ship. Nikki sat up and waved.

"Sorry I took so long to get here," said Linnea, sitting down on the grass beside them. "I thought it best to take as many back roads as possible after I left the tournament, to be sure I wasn't followed." She folded back a red-and-white checked cloth which covered the basket she'd been carrying. A delicious smell of just-baked bread wafted up from it. "I'm sure you two are ravenous. I've got a stew simmering on the stove, but this should tide you over until it's ready." She pried the top off a jar of jam and spread it on a thick slice of warm bread. "Blueberry," she said, handing the bread to Nikki. "I had a spectacular crop this year. We're practically drowning in blueberries here. I tried out a new method of fertilization and it worked like a charm." She handed Gwen a slice of bread and bit into one herself. Rosie scampered down from her head and nibbled at the crumbs Linnea held in her palm.

Out of the corner of her eye Nikki noticed that her rucksack, which she'd dropped on the lawn beside her, was writhing like a python. She snatched up Cation just in time, grabbing the kitten by the scruff of the neck as she shot out of the rucksack and launched herself at Rosie.

Rosie squeaked in terror and dived into Linnea's sleeve. Linnea raised her arm protectively, cupping her elbow where Rosie was huddled inside her sleeve in a trembling lump. "I wasn't aware you had a cat," she said, eyeing Cation with a hint of unfriendliness. "As a rule I don't allow them here. Rosie is not my only pet. I also have a chipmunk called Nutter and a parrot called Samson. Your kitten could seriously injure them. Though old Samson would put up a good fight. He's got quite a vicious bite when he's cranky, which is most of the time."

"I think I can manage it so that Nikki's kitten isn't a problem," said Gwen. She tore a long skinny strip off the hem of her dress and quickly fashioned a little harness. She slipped it over Cation's head and around her chest, tightening it just enough so that the kitten couldn't squirm out of it. "There," she said. "As long as she's on her leash she shouldn't be a danger to your animals."

Cation growled and blinked up at Gwen with a petulant expression, as if to say she'd be a danger to anything she liked, but eventually she quieted down and curled up in Nikki's lap. She let Nikki feed her pieces of jam-covered bread while she kept a sharp eye on Linnea's elbow and hissed softly.

"Really wonderful jam," said Gwen, wiping her mouth.

Linnea nodded. "Yes, as I said, we had bushels of blueberries this year. I've sold hundreds of jars of jam at the market in Kingston. It was dried cow's dung which produced such a large crop. I put it around the roots of the blueberry bushes and they grew much faster than usual. I believe there is something in the dung which causes plants to grow."

"Nitrogen," said Nikki, licking her jam-covered fingers. "It increases plant size and the amount of fruit a bush will produce." She was now mentally checking practically everything she said while in the Realm of Reason, but she didn't see how any harm could come from mentioning nitrogen to Linnea and Gwen. It wasn't a harmful element like uranium or a valuable one like gold. Avaricious and

Fortuna had tried to force her to produce gold from lead, but she seriously doubted that there was anyone in Kingston who was desperate to produce more cow manure. "It's one of the elements in the Periodic Table, a type of classification system we've developed in my land which describes the properties of metals, metalloids, the Noble Gases, and other elements. Nitrogen is element number seven in the table, and cow manure contains a lot of it. Gardeners and farmers in my land use manure to help plants grow. We call it fertilizer."

Linnea was looking at Nikki in such surprise that Gwen laughed. "You'll have to excuse Nikki," she said. "She suffers from the same disease I do: obsession with alchemy."

"Chemistry," said Nikki. "We call it chemistry in my land."

Gwen nodded. "Chemistry. Yes, you told me that back in my basement laboratory in Muddled Manor." She sighed. "I sometimes wish I was back there. Mother is a pain, but I do miss my lovely laboratory. All my distillation glassware that took me years to collect. I hope mother hasn't thrown it all out. I was quite surprised when I left home and went to work in Avaricious's shop in Deceptionville. I had expected such a large business to have an extensive laboratory, but mine was much better than Avaricious's."

Linnea chuckled. "Good old Avaricious. Such a greedy lump of lard, strutting around Deceptionville, obsessed with getting rich. I suppose I shouldn't laugh. He treats his workers terribly. Like slaves. Though I have to admit I do love to browse in his shop. He has such a wonderful collection of dried herbs from all over the Realm and even some from the Southern Isles."

"That's how Linnea and I know each other," said Gwen to Nikki. "I was working in Avaricious's shop one day, distilling an essence of lavender, when Linnea came in and asked for nightshade root. One of the other workers heard her and ran out of the shop to find a Rounder. Linnea nearly got arrested. I had to hustle her out the back door."

"Why?" asked Nikki.

"Nightshade's a deadly poison," said Linnea. "The Rounders keep track of who buys it, probably so someone doesn't use it to poison the Deceptionville town council, not that that would be a very great loss. They're a bunch of bribe-taking moochers. Anyway, nightshade is very difficult to grow, so I have to buy it. I make a special trip to Deceptionville every year just for it. Avaricious's shop is one of the only places in the Realm which has it. I bought a few seeds of it last year from a trader from the Southern Isles, but I wasn't able to cultivate the plant. The seeds won't sprout in this climate."

"But if it's poisonous why would you want it?" asked Nikki.

"It causes numbness and sleepiness in small doses," said Linnea. "I often get local farmers calling on me when one of their children has broken an arm or leg. I have some skill in setting broken bones. In addition to my work with plants I have long studied the bones of small animals such as the mice and foxes which have died in my fields. Their skeletal structures are fascinating. Each type of animal has a different skeleton, yet they all share basic components such as a backbone. From studying the skeletons I learned how the different bones joined together and how to splint them when they were broken. I started helping lame dogs, but soon found that the same type of setting and splinting would work on humans. I give the injured animal or person a small dose of nightshade root steeped in water. They fall into a deep sleep and I am able to set their broken bone without causing them pain. It works much better than the old practice of giving them alcohol. Drunk people can still feel pain. But I have to be very careful with the dosage when I use nightshade. Give too much and you can easily kill your patient. I had Dolor, the local Toothpuller, come around last month asking me for some, but I had to refuse. He's not the most reliable person. When he's wielding his pliers on someone's tooth he's usually as drunk as his patient. You should see the bloody mess he makes of people's mouths. He definitely isn't capable of carefully measuring a dose of nightshade."

"Instead of getting his patients drunk he could try numbing the nerve of the tooth," said Nikki, whose skin was crawling at the thought of someone with pliers yanking out one of her teeth. She'd always hated going to the dentist, but at that moment she was intensely grateful for modern dentistry and its needles full of Novocain.

"What is a nerve?" asked Linnea.

"It's a kind of pathway in the body which transmits pain," replied Nikki. Her mind was spinning with worry again about what to say next. She was having the same kind of debate with herself that she'd had back in the Prince's old laboratory in the Southern Castle. How much modern knowledge should she introduce to the Realm of Reason? Obviously anything which could be used to create weapons was out of the question, but what about medical knowledge which might help ease suffering? Not that medicine was a subject she knew much about. Chemistry was more her thing. But her AP Biology class had included some basic human anatomy. When they'd discussed nerve endings and various ways to ease pain her teacher had mentioned that coca was chemically similar to Novocain. It had been used by dentists back in the nineteenth century to help with tooth pain. Her teacher had even given them a basic description of how coca was extracted from the leaves of the coca tree, something which had nearly gotten him fired. Did the Realm of Reason have something similar to a coca tree?

"You mentioned that you bought some nightshade seeds from a trader from the Southern Isles," said Nikki. "Did you buy any other plants from him?"

Linnea nodded. "I always buy a little of whatever he has, whether I need it or not. It's a long journey from the Southern Isles and he doesn't come around here very often."

"These Southern Isles," said Nikki, "are they tropical?"

Linnea frowned. "Tropical? I'm not familiar with the word."

"It means a place which is hot and rainy, with lots of jungles. Lots of vines and snakes and trees which are different from the pines and oaks you have here."

"Yes, that sounds like the Southern Isles," said Linnea. "I've never been there myself, but I've heard sailors at the port in Kingston say that the air in the Southern Isles is so full of water that a person can hardly breathe, and that there are vines hanging from the trees as thick as your arm."

Nikki nodded. She had come to a decision. She was going to try to introduce a new painkilling technique to the Realm of Reason. It just seemed like the right thing to do, though she wished that an adult like her biology teacher or her mother was there to advise her. Maybe she was making a mistake, but she couldn't get the horrible picture of the local tooth-puller out of her mind. She might have an opportunity to save people a lot of pain and it seemed wrong not to try. "Let's go take a look at the plants you've collected from the Southern Isles," she said.

Linnea looked a little surprised, but she shrugged good-naturedly and gathered up her basket, cradling her elbow where the lump which was Rosie still trembled.

Nikki racked her brain as she scooped up Cation and followed Gwen and Linnea across the lawn toward Linnea's thatched-roof house. She was trying to remember that day back in her biology class when her teacher had talked about nerve pain and dentistry. What was the guy's name? Halsted? That sounded right. William Halsted. Sometime in the 1880's he'd used coca as a local anesthetic during a dental procedure. He'd used a four percent solution of coca in alcohol, injected with a hypodermic needle into the patient's gum near the tooth he was going to pull. She was pretty sure she could remember the steps her nearly-fired teacher had described for getting coca out of coca leaves. Her process would be crude, as she didn't have access to sophisticated lab equipment, but she was pretty sure she could produce a workable painkiller. If it worked it would be much safer than the nightshade Linnea used. Since Linnea's patients swallowed the nightshade it affected their whole body. The coca-leaf concoction she hoped to produce would be injected, affecting only one nerve next to one tooth. The patient would never be unconscious the way they were with nightshade, so they would never be in danger of having their heart or breathing stop. A pang of doubt suddenly stopped her in her tracks. Coca was extremely addictive. She didn't want to be responsible for creating drug addicts in the Realm of Reason.

"Nikki? Are you all right?" asked Gwen, looking back at her.

Nikki looked up, surprised to find herself standing in the doorway of Linnea's house. She gave Gwen a reassuring smile. "Sure. I'm fine. Just thinking over some stuff." She stepped into the main room of the house. It was a sturdy, comforting room, with thick stone walls and a huge fireplace with a mantel blackened with soot.

Linnea set her basket down on the heavy oak dining table in the middle of the room and proceeded down the hall into a pantry next to the kitchen. A whiff of sulfur wafted through the air as she scratched a match against the stone wall and lit a candle to light the cool, dark room. "I have quite a collection, as you can see," she said, sweeping her hand around the room. It was lined floor to ceiling with shelves. "I've been collecting dried plants, herbs, and seeds since I was a child. I've lost count, but I must have over a thousand different kinds." She led them to a row of shelves against one wall. "These are from the Southern Isles."

Nikki peered into the clay pots and straw baskets filled with seeds and dried plants. She'd seen coca leaves in person once. A girl who'd emigrated from Peru had brought some of the leaves into her biology class. She'd told the class that Peruvians living high up in the Andes Mountains chewed the coca leaves as a remedy for altitude sickness.

She'd passed the leaves around the class and Nikki had tried one. The leaf had an unpleasant, bitter taste and had left her mouth feeling numb. As near as she could remember the leaf had been small, oblong, and dark green . . . Nikki picked a leaf out of a clay pot and sniffed it. No, the smell was too sweet. She nibbled on one from a reed basket. No, the taste was wrong. She sniffed another candidate. Maybe. She broke off a tiny piece and cautiously chewed it. Yes, this might be it. The same bitter taste, the same mild numbness on her tongue.

"Can I take a few of these?" she asked.

"Certainly, if you wish," said Linnea. "They're just gathering dust. I've never figured out a use for them. The trader I bought them from said the islanders boil them to make a tea. I tried that but it tasted terrible."

"In my land we don't use this for tea," said Nikki. "We make a kind of painkiller from it."

Linnea's eyes widened. "Really? How interesting. Can you show me how to make it? I'm always looking for better ways to help the local villagers with their health problems. And they would be thrilled with anything which makes the Toothpuller's visits less painful."

Nikki nodded. "I was thinking exactly the same thing. I'm not sure I can do it, but if my idea works it will be much better than giving your patients alcohol or nightshade."

Chapter Three

◀ ●● ▶

The Toothpuller

NIKKI BLEW OUT the flame burning on the wick of an oil lamp. A small clay pot rested on an iron trestle above the lamp, its bottom warm from the flame. A wisp of steam floated above the liquid in the pot. Nikki sniffed it. The concentrated liquid still had tiny pieces of leaves floating in it, but she was pretty sure it was at least a four percent solution of coca in alcohol. It might even be a bit stronger. The only way to be sure was to test it. And that presented its own problems, especially the problem of the delivery system. The Realm was unlikely to have hypodermic needles, but that was the best way of getting her solution close enough to a nerve. Just rubbing it on a patient's gums or having them swish it in their mouth wasn't going to be enough. She was just pouring the solution into a small glass jar and sealing the jar with a cork when she heard familiar voices out in the main room of the house. She set the jar on a shelf and rushed out of the pantry.

"Miss! You are all right! We were so worried!" Athena ran up to Nikki and grabbed her hand, squeezing it tightly. The imp had shed her bulky Seeker robes and was once again in her prim grey dress, which was unwrinkled and spotless despite her journey.

Nikki bent down and gave the imp a quick hug. "I'm fine. So is Gwen."

Fuzz gave her a cheeky wink. He had also disposed of his robes and was back in his usual trousers, shirt and embroidered vest, none of which was spotless and all of which smelled of ale. "Of course you're fine. I told Miss Worrywart to stop her fussing, but she was sure you were all dead in a ditch somewhere or locked away in the deepest dungeon of the Southern Castle. A place, by the way, which I happen to have a personal acquaintance with. I'm afraid I can't recommend the accommodations. The beds are flea-covered piles of hay and the rats are way too friendly. I don't mind rats when they know their place, but their place is not inside my pant leg."

"Hello, Miss" mumbled Curio through a mouthful of jam-smeared bread. He was sitting on a faded armchair near the fireplace, his thin legs hovering a foot off the floor. He still had on his Seeker robe. He raised this a few inches to reveal a pair of brown linen trousers. "Look, Miss. Mr. Fuzz got me brand new clothes! Never had new clothes before. Makes me feel quite fancy. And I can tell they're good quality, cause of how much they itch."

"Time for dinner," announced Linnea, swooping into the room, a pile of plates in one hand and a basket of bread in the other. She and her cook quickly set the table. The cook was a grumpy man built like a bulldog who scowled at everyone as if daring them to eat anything he'd made. The gardeners and farmhands who worked Linnea's lands came in and they were all about to tuck into a huge pot of stew and piles of fresh-baked bread with just-churned butter when a piercing scream came from outside the front door.

They all jumped up from the table. The front door banged open and a small boy rushed in, screaming at the top of his lungs. He ran to Linnea and hid behind her, clutching desperately at her skirt.

"Don't let him near me, Miss," shrieked the boy. "He'll tear my whole head off with those pinchers of his. I swear he will."

"I'm not going ta tear your head off, you stupid brat. Just yer teeth."

Nikki had to bite back a scream herself when the man who had spoken stepped through the doorway. He looked like a dead person who had thrown back the lid of his coffin and walked into his own funeral. He was well over six feet tall, with skin the color of spoiled milk. His skull-like head held teeth so black they looked like pieces of coal. In one hand he held a pair of pliers. Their tip was coated with something that looked suspiciously like blood.

"Hello Dolor," said Linnea calmly. "I see you're still plying your trade."

Dolor grinned wickedly, the stench of alcohol streaming from his rotting teeth. "Aye, and I'll keep doing it long as it pays. Which it does." He pointed his bloody pliers at the boy shivering behind Linnea. "This one's parents are paying me two gold coins, real gold, mind you, to yank out 'is front teeth. And no amount of 'is screeching is goin ta keep me from my pay."

Linnea frowned and knelt down in front of the little boy, gently taking his jaw in her hand. "Open your mouth, sweetheart. Let me take a quick look."

Tears sprouted from the boy's eyes, but he nodded and slowly opened his mouth.

Nikki gasped and put a hand over her mouth. The smell was so strong she thought for a moment she was going to vomit. I was a smell she recognized. One she would never forget. When she was six she'd had an abscessed tooth. It had become infected and her mother had taken her to the dentist to have it pulled out. She'd screamed so much that the dentist had had to put her under. When she'd woken up there was a bloody hole in her mouth that she kept poking her tongue into. The dentist had given her antibiotics for the infection, but she'd never forgotten the smell.

"Oh, honey," said Linnea softly. "I'm so sorry, but those two front teeth of yours definitely need to come out. They're both rotten."

"But, but," sobbed the little boy, "they'll fall out by themselves. I know they will. All the kids in my village have had their teeth fall out."

Linnea nodded. "You're right, they're baby teeth, but I'm afraid we can't wait for yours to fall out naturally. If we don't pull them out right now you'll get very sick. You might even die."

Dolor advanced on the little boy, snapping his bloody pliers. "Time for me ta earn me pay." He gestured at the cook. "Plop 'im in that chair by the fire and hold 'im down. Hold 'im down good, specially his legs. Yesterday one of the little brats I was workin' on kicked me right in me privates."

The cook stepped toward the little boy, but Nikki blocked his way. "Wait," she said. "You can't just yank out his teeth. The pain will be terrible."

Dolor shrugged. "Pain's part of life. And it's specially part of tooth-pullin'." He grinned and snapped his pliers at the boy.

"Nikki's right," said Linnea. "We can at least ease his suffering before you start yanking. I'll get my nightshade mixture."

Linnea snatched a candle from the mantelpiece and hurried out of the room. Nikki followed.

"I don't have much nightshade left," said Linnea as she rushed into the pantry and snatched up a tiny glass bottle with a wax stopper. "But it should be enough to put the child under. It won't take much. He's very small. Normally I don't like to give nightshade to children that tiny. It overwhelms their system and can stop their breathing. But I just can't stand by while Dolor tortures the poor child."

Nikki put a hand on her arm. "I have a better solution. I hope" She retrieved the solution of coca leaves in alcohol she had distilled. "This is the painkiller I was talking about. We use it in my land to numb a tooth before pulling it. I believe it will ease the boy's pain without having to knock him unconscious with nightshade. It will be much safer."

Linnea took the bottle from her and held it up to the candlelight. A few bits of green leaves swirled in the cloudy liquid. She gave Nikki a doubtful look. "Are you sure about this? Will it really work as you say?"

"Yes," said Nikki with much more confidence than she felt. "I just need a delivery system."

Linnea looked at her in confusion.

"A needle," said Nikki. "A very, very thin one. In my land we use what we call a hypodermic needle to inject the painkiller into the tooth, but you don't have those here so we'll have to use a regular needle. It won't work quite as well, and we'll probably have to jab the boy's tooth multiple times unfortunately. That will hurt, but not as much as having his teeth yanked out by the roots without any painkiller at all."

Linnea looked at her thoughtfully. "We need to jab his tooth?"

Nikki nodded. "Down below the gum line. At the bottom of the tooth, where the root is."

Linnea handed Nikki the bottle of coca solution and reached up to the top shelf again. She took down a small wooden box and opened its lid. "Nightshade paste," she said. "It's my nightshade solution in concentrated form, with all the water evaporated. I mix it with a little beeswax to keep it soft. I use it when someone has a small cut or puncture wound. It numbs the skin for several hours, making the wound less painful. I was thinking, if we rub the boy's gums with this before you jab him with the needle it will make the jabs less painful. And since he won't be swallowing it there's not much danger that it will cause him to stop breathing."

"Yes, that's a very good idea," said Nikki, trying to smile at Linnea, though her hands trembled and her stomach jolted. It had never occurred to her that *she* would be the one doing the jabbing. She'd assumed that Linnea would be the one wielding the needle. Before she knew it Linnea had plucked a needle from a sewing kit in a corner of the pantry and was leading her back to the main room.

The little boy was huddled in the armchair in front of the fire,

Curio's arm protectively circling his shoulders.

"Curio," said Nikki, "why don't you go and sit at the table. Have some stew."

Curio's normally cheerful face turned stormy. "I won't, Miss, begging your pardon. He's in an awful amount of pain, he is. I won't let anyone pull out his teeth just for sport."

Nikki crossed her arms and assumed what she hoped was a Mom-like expression. "Curio, you know very well that I'd never hurt anyone just for fun. We have to do this or he'll die. It's as simple as that. Now go to the table and eat your dinner."

Curio reluctantly slid off the chair and backed away a few feet.

Nikki didn't want him watching this, but she didn't have time to argue with him. Her hands were already starting to shake. If she waited any longer her nerves would get the better of her and it would be impossible to do what needed to be done. She nodded at Linnea.

Linnea knelt down in front of the chair and gently opened the boy's mouth. She dipped her finger in the nightshade paste and rubbed it into the gums near the boy's two front teeth. The boy winced and hastily wiped away a tear, but he didn't resist.

"It works quickly," said Linnea, getting to her feet. "Go ahead."

Nikki nodded, her heart racing. She knelt in front of the chair and peered into the boy's mouth, her already churning stomach becoming even more nauseous from the smell. She pulled the stopper off her bottle of coca solution and dipped Linnea's needle in it. Hypodermic needles were hollow. When her dentist back home pushed the plunger the Novocain was forced through the hollow needle and into her gum. Since she didn't have a hypodermic needle her plan was to jab the gum and let the solution run down the outside of the needle. The amount of solution she could administer this way was small, so she'd need multiple jabs to thoroughly numb each tooth. With one shaking hand she gently pricked the gum just above the boy's front teeth.

Linnea laid a hand on Nikki's shoulder. "You'll need to jab harder, I'm afraid. You aren't doing the boy any favors by holding back."

Nikki nodded, a tear running down her cheek. This was one of the hardest things she'd ever had to do. She dipped the needle in the solution again and held the boy's chin with her other hand. This time she plunged the needle in until it wouldn't go in any farther. She watched as the liquid ran down the side of the needle and into the tiny hole she'd made.

After five more jabs Nikki stood up, her legs trembling. "I think that will do it."

Dolor grunted and advanced on the boy. "Bout time. Ain't got all day. Don't know why we're messing about with silly needles anyways. The boy's not a pincushion."

"Wait!" said Nikki. "The painkiller will take a few minutes to work. You can't pull his teeth just yet. And before you do I insist that you wash your pliers. They're so dirty you'll give the boy an infection."

Dolor glared at her, but Linnea nodded. "Quite right," she said. "Hand them over." She held out her palm.

Dolor's skull-like face darkened, but he finally handed over his pliers and retreated to the table, where he began eating stew straight out of the pot with his fingers.

Nikki followed Linnea into the kitchen. In one corner a small hole had been cut into the thick stone wall and a clay pipe jutted out. Water trickled from the pipe into a wooden barrel.

"The village stonecutter arranged this for me last year," said Linnea, sticking the bloody pliers under the running water. "It's quite handy. Before this was in place we used to have to carry buckets of water in from the well outside in the yard."

Nikki watched as blood dripped off the pliers into the barrel. "I hope you aren't going to drink this water," she said.

Linnea shook her head and pointed down at the floor. Another pipe ran out of the bottom of the barrel and back outside through another hole in the wall. "The drain is open. The dirty water will run out of the barrel and into a trench which runs the length of the house. Once the dirty water is flushed out I'll close the drain and we'll have clean drinking water again. Darius, that's our stonecutter, is quite an ingenious person. I'm thinking of introducing him to Gwendolyn. They both have the same kind of curious and innovative mind. I think they would get along very well, if you know what I mean." She winked playfully at Nikki. "Matchmaking isn't really my area of expertise, so I can't make any promises." She held the wet pliers up to the light from the open window. "That's as clean as this instrument of torture is going to get, I think. Best get this over with, for the boy's sake. The waiting can be the worst part, sometimes."

"Wait," said Nikki. "Do you have any alcohol?"

Linnea raised an eyebrow. "Alcohol? Aren't you a bit young to be drinking?"

"It's not for me," said Nikki. "It's for the pliers. To kill the germs."

"The what?" asked Linnea.

"The germs," said Nikki. "The bacteria. Even though the pliers look clean, I bet there's still millions of bacteria still on it. Alcohol can kill them."

Linnea looked at her like she'd lost her mind. "There's nothing on the pliers. See?" She held them up to the light of the sunset coming through the window.

"Bacteria are invisible to the naked eye. You'd need a microscope to see them." She waved her hand impatiently as Linnea started to say something. "I'll explain later. The boy's teeth should be numb by now. If we wait too long the painkiller will start to wear off." She glanced at the shelves lining the kitchen walls. "You must have some kind of alcohol here. Not ale or wine. Something clear, like vodka."

Linnea took a bottle down from a shelf. "I don't know what vodka is, but this is grain alcohol. We make it from barley."

Nikki nodded and took the bottle. "That should work." She uncorked the bottle and held the pliers over a basin sitting on the big wooden work table in the middle of the kitchen. She poured a good-sized helping of the alcohol over the pliers. "There, that should zap most of the germs." She handed the pliers back to Linnea. "If you don't mind, I think I'll wait here until Dolor has finished."

Linnea patted her on the shoulder. "Of course. You've done wonderfully well, my dear. I know it was difficult for you. Believe me, when I first started setting broken bones, many years ago, I was far more of a wreck than you are now. I would throw up, both before the procedure and after it." She hurried out of the kitchen with the pliers.

Nikki bent over the stone countertop which ran along one wall and rested her forehead on its cold surface. She held her hands over her ears, ready for the screams, but none came. After what seemed like hours but was probably only a few minutes she heard voices coming toward the kitchen.

Nikki lifted her head from the counter and saw the little boy with the rotten teeth standing in the doorway. There was blood dripping from his chin, but he was smiling. He rushed forward and took Nikki's hand.

"Look," he said, pointing at the gaping hole in his mouth where his two front teeth had been. "And it didn't even hurt. Miss Linnea says that you stopped the pain with your needles. It was like magic. Are you a wizard?"

Nikki laughed. "No, I'm not a wizard. I'm a scientist. At least, I want to be, when I'm older. My Mom's a scientist, and I want to be just like her."

"I want to be a scientist too," said the boy. "I don't know what a scientist is, but that's what I'm going to be when I grow up."

Nikki laughed again. "A scientist is someone who studies the natural world. Like Linnea. She studies plants and animal bones and farming. She's what my people would call a biologist. She's kind of like a bard of Biology."

The boy nodded solemnly and wiped the blood off his chin. "That's what I want to be. A Bard of Biology. I'll ask Miss Linnea if I can 'prentice with her. I was 'sposed to 'prentice with a pig farmer in the next village, but being a Bard of Biology is much better than being a pig farmer."

"Prentice?" asked Nikki.

"Get trained up," said the boy. "You live with your master and get trained up so that when you're old enough you can take over and do the job yourself."

"Oh, right," said Nikki. "An apprenticeship. Yes, that's a very good idea."

"I'll go ask Miss Linnea right now," said the boy. He made Nikki a funny little bow and ran out of the kitchen.

End of Excerpt

Excerpt from Hamsters Rule, Gerbils Drool

Chapter One

MELVIN STIRRED UNEASILY in his pile of sawdust shavings. The snuffly snores coming from the twin bed across the room were disturbing his rest. He crawled out of his nest and trundled down an orange plastic tunnel to a distant corner of his Hamster Habitat. Diving head first into a pile of cedar chips, he squirmed until only his chubby rear-end was visible. He twitched for a few seconds then settled back into sleep.

Melvin should have counted himself lucky. The snores of his owner, Miss Sally Jane Hesslop, who was eleven years old as of last Tuesday, were much quieter than usual due to Sally's head being buried under her *Xena Warrior Princess* bedspread. All that could be seen of Sally was a long strand of blonde hair with a wad of pink bubble gum stuck on the end of it.

The morning sun finished clearing the fog from San Francisco bay and lit up Sally's bedroom window. The light revealed quite a mess: Legos, comic books, sneakers, mismatched socks and a spilled can of Hungry Hamster Snacks were scattered across the floor. Sally was a firm believer in keeping all of her belongings in plain view. In an emergency (and most mornings were an emergency, as Sally had a talent for being late for school) precious time could be saved by getting dressed from the clothes on the floor.

This morning Sally's peaceful slumber was destined to last only a few more brief moments, for Robbie was out of bed and on the loose.

Robbie was Sally's four-year-old brother. He was famous up and down their neighborhood for his ability to eat anything dirt-related. Mud, clay, sand, litter box filler, anything lurking in the bottom of a flowerpot or fish tank, all were fair game. When it came to dirt Robbie was an omnivore. Though, of course, he had his favorites. The light fluffiness at the heart of the vacuum cleaner bag, the tasty compost at the roots of his grandmother's roses – these were special treats for special occasions, to be savored slowly and washed down with a good quality grape Kool Aid.

Today Robbie was up at his usual time of six a.m. He tiptoed into Sally's room, a stealthy menace in his footie pajamas and bike helmet. This helmet was a permanent item in Robbie's wardrobe. Robbie was fond of banging his head on things in a rhythmic pattern similar to certain popular hip-hop songs, so his father had started putting a helmet on him as soon as Robbie got out of bed.

Giggling softly and wielding a large rubber spatula, Robbie crept up to the snoring Sally. He pulled back the edge of the bedspread with one chubby fist and brought the spatula down with a satisfying thwhack on top of Sally's head.

"Aaaah!" Sally bolted upright, her scrawny arms swinging wildly as she tried to ward off her assailant. Her oversized *Xena* T-shirt billowed out, making her eighty-pound frame look twice its size. A neon-yellow post-it note which was stuck to her forehead fluttered in the breeze as she whipped around and grabbed the spatula from a chortling Robbie. Sally rained down a barrage of blows with the spatula onto Robbie's bike helmet. Robbie made a dash for the door, knocking over a stack of comic books. He was almost to safety, inches from escape, when he miscalculated the distance between the door jamb and his head. He bounced backwards off the door, his helmet taking most of the punishment, tripped over a half-built castle made of Legos, and toppled over onto the carpet with his feet in the air.

Sally leapt out of bed with a wild war cry and rained rubbery blows down on Robbie as if beating a stubborn batch of dough.

"Sally Jane, are you out of bed yet?" The voice floating in from the hallway sounded in desperate need of coffee. Sally's father's dearest dream was to sleep in past six a.m., a dream which was destroyed on a daily basis by Robbie and his spatula. Robbie had assigned himself the task of family alarm clock and he took his job seriously. If the first whack on the head didn't wake his target at six on the dot then Robbie would tirelessly whack until he got results. Mr. Hesslop had tried hiding the spatula in the back of the cereal cupboard, but Robbie had just switched to whacking with the toilet brush. Mr. Hesslop had quickly decided that he preferred the spatula, the toilet brush tending to catch in his hair.

Sally gave Robbie one final blow then grabbed his pajama feet and dragged him out of her room. "I'm up, Dad. I'm up," she shouted, leaving Robbie lying on his back in the hallway. Sally darted back into her room and slammed the door. She yawned, scratched her ear with the captured spatula, and surveyed her wardrobe. Her favorite pair of jeans, only slightly muddy around the knees, hung off the end of her bed. She pulled them on and selected a pink T-shirt from a pile under the window. As she pulled it over her head the post-it which was stuck to her forehead fluttered to the floor. Sally scooped it up and read it aloud.

"Charlie Sanderson must pay. Skedyul revenge for recess."

Sally's blue eyes narrowed to slits, and she smacked her palm with the spatula.

"Right. It's payday, Charlie. Today, after third period."

"Okay, Robbie. You've had enough. Come and drink your juice."

Robbie, crouching over a scraggly fern which an aunt had given them for Christmas, ignored his Dad. He reached into the depths of the flowerpot and pulled up a fistful of loamy soil. He carefully picked off a ladybug which was crawling toward his thumb and then crammed the dirt into his mouth.

Mr. Hesslop sighed. He grabbed Robbie off the floor and plopped him into a chair at the kitchen table. Mr. Hesslop was a taller version of Sally Jane. Both father and daughter had dishwater blond hair, blue eyes, long skinny arms and legs, and pointy elbows. Short, chubby Robbie, with his dark hair and brown eyes, looked completely unrelated to his Dad and his eleven-year-old sister, a fact which Sally mercilessly exploited. She had convinced Robbie that he was on loan from the bank that their Dad worked at, and that he could be returned at any time if she just said the word. Robbie had responded to this threat by reducing Sally's spatula wake-up calls to once a week. His Dad still got the seven-day-a-week treatment though, Robbie guessing correctly that his Dad loved him too much to pack him up and store him in a bank vault.

"Robbie, you've got to stop eating dirt." Mr. Hesslop grabbed a paper napkin and wiped Robbie's muddy mouth. "Remember what Dr. Tompkins told you? If you don't stop you're going to have a tree growing in there." He tickled Robbie's stomach.

Robbie giggled. "Tree in tummy."

Sally wandered into the kitchen, bumping into the refrigerator. Her long, straight hair hung in front of her face like a curtain. She had attempted to braid pieces of it, and the attempt had not gone well. One braid sprouted from the top of her head like an overgrown onion. Another looked like it was growing straight out of her ear. She sat down at the kitchen table, one hand tangled in the rest of her unbraided hair, the other grabbing for a box of Cheerios.

Mr. Hesslop passed her the milk. "Sally Jane, why don't you let me help you with your hair? I'll make you look real pretty."

What could be seen of Sally's face under her hair looked suspiciously like it was rolling its eyes. "Daaad. I'm not trying to look *pretty*. I'm doing Xena braids. See, if you're in a fight you don't want your hair in your face. You can't see good."

"What fight?" Mr. Hesslop said sharply, his thin nose pointed at his daughter like a fox on the scent.

Sally smiled innocently. "I was just being hypometical, Dad. Sheesh."

"Hypothetical," said Mr. Hesslop. "Robbie, don't do that." He grabbed Robbie's juice glass, which was now half empty. Robbie had poured the rest onto the floor and was straining against his father's arm, eager to get down from the table to study (and taste) the effects of orange juice on dirty linoleum at close range.

Melvin waddled into the kitchen, his fluffy orange fur dusting a path along the un-swept floor, his nose twitching for food. He disappeared under Sally's chair, dodged her swinging feet, and settled in front of the puddle of orange juice. His tiny pink tongue darted out and lapped at lightning speed, aware that even Mr. Hesslop with his lazy housekeeping skills was unlikely to leave a bonanza like this lying around for long.

Fortunately for Melvin, Mr. Hesslop was distracted by the sound of a knock at the front door. He set Robbie down and went to greet their visitor. A few seconds later he reappeared with Darlene Trockworthy, their next-door neighbor. A peroxide blond with heavy blue eye-shadow, a too-tight dress and too-high heels, Darlene occasionally babysat Robbie and Sally. Darlene and Robbie were best friends, mainly because Darlene let Robbie eat as much dirt as he wanted, but between Darlene and Sally it had been war from the start.

Darlene slid into a seat at the kitchen table, aiming a kick at Melvin on the way. "Is that rat loose again?" she asked, her mouth full of the toast she had grabbed off of Robbie's plate.

Sally glared at her. "He's not a rat, you dingbat."

"Sally, watch your manners," Mr. Hesslop said sharply.

"Bill, the kid's rhyming again. I thought you said she'd grow out of that." Darlene pouted at Mr. Hesslop, her bright red lipstick spattered with toast crumbs. The whole neighborhood knew that Darlene had her "sights set" on Bill Hesslop, but so far he had resisted her advances.

"She'll grow out of it eventually," said Mr. Hesslop. "It's just a phase. Robbie, don't do that."

Robbie had climbed off his chair and was sitting on the floor, rubbing Cheerios in the dust on the floor before eating them.

Mr. Hesslop picked him up. "I'll clean up Mr. Dirt Devil here and drop him at his preschool. Can you take Sally?"

The look Darlene shot Sally clearly said that she'd like to dump Sally in San Francisco bay. Darlene sighed heavily. "Yeah, sure." She pointed a warning finger at Sally, a long red fingernail raking the air like a claw. "But no rhyming, kid. I mean it. One Iambic what-ya-ma-callit and I'm selling you to the slave traders. They'll ship you to Nebraska and make you shuck corn 'til you're eighty."

Sally smiled at her sweetly. "Your wish is my command. And your head is filled with sand." Sally scooped Melvin up, put him on her shoulder, and marched out of the kitchen.

"Put that rat back in his cage." Darlene yelled after her. "And if you're not ready in ten minutes I'm leaving without you."

Chapter Two

S ALLY AND DARLENE maintained a careful no-touching distance as they headed down the hill to Sally's school. When a bike rider on the sidewalk forced them to shrink the gap between them they automatically sprang apart again after the bike had passed, as if repelled by a magnetic field.

Darlene examined her makeup in a compact mirror as she teetered along, causing oncoming pedestrians to grumble as they jumped out of her way. Sally practiced karate kicks, viciously attacking the most dangerous looking trash cans and mailboxes along their route, her backpack flopping wildly on her shoulders.

Halfway down the hill a posse of poodles suddenly rushed out the front door of a tall apartment building and made straight for Sally. Sally threw herself down on her knees and scooped up the scruffy little white poodle which was leading the pack. The little poodle yapped excitedly, licking Sally's face. The other three poodles were tall, black, and dignified, with the fur on their heads shaped into elegant topknots. They sniffed at Sally's backpack and at Darlene's shoes. One of them lifted his leg and took aim at Darlene's stiletto. Darlene shrieked and jumped back.

"Brutus! No!"

A chubby little girl about Sally's age ran up to them and grabbed the peeing poodle. She had black curly hair and large dark eyes. She was wearing a plaid skirt, a starched white blouse, and black patent leather shoes which looked extremely uncomfortable. "Brutus, you bad dog! Sorry, Miss Trockworthy. My Mom's trying to train him not to pee on everyone, but he forgets sometimes." She herded the poodles back up the front steps of the apartment building. "C'mon Brutus, Caesar, Nero, and Fluffy. You can't come to school with us. Poodles are not allowed. Go back upstairs."

Sally waved goodbye to Fluffy and stood up, dusting off her knees. "Hi, Katie! Are you ready to rumble?"

The chubby girl looked at her in confusion. "Huh?"

Sally skipped around Katie, chanting. "Charlie's a boy, so he's not too bright. We'll shout with joy when we win this fight."

Katie picked up the book bag she had dropped during the poodle roundup. A worried frown crinkled her pale forehead. "I don't know, Sally. Remember what happened the last time you got into a fight at school? Billy Lauder's tooth got knocked out and Arnold the Iguana ate it and had to go to the Pet Hospital. I don't want Arnold to go to the Pet Hospital. He doesn't like it there. Remember the time I put my Mom's Lilac Mist hand lotion on him because he looked dry? I thought it would make him feel better, but it turned him all pink and he had to go to the Pet Hospital so they could make him green again. Arnold hates being pink. Pink is a girl's color, and Arnold's a boy iguana. Mr. Zukas says so. So you shouldn't fight."

Katie looked ready to cry. Her large eyes grew red-rimmed and shiny. Sally patted her on the shoulder and handed her a wadded up Kleenex which she pulled out of her backpack. She resumed skipping in circles.

"Arnold's not going to the Pet Hospital this time," said Sally. "I have a new Secret Revenge Plan, and there aren't any iguanas in the plan."

Katie sniffed and wiped her nose. She followed Sally and Darlene as they continued down the hill. "Oh. Well, I guess it's okay then. I'm glad Arnold isn't in your new Secret Revenge Plan, 'cause iguanas don't like fighting. They're pacifiers."

Sally stopped skipping and nodded knowingly. "Iguanas are pacifiers cause they can't do karate kicks." She demonstrated a karate kick, narrowly missing the nose of a passing Pomeranian. The Pomeranian growled at her and Sally growled back.

They reached the bottom of the hill and turned onto a narrow side street lined with gingko trees. The sidewalk was covered with fan-shaped gingko leaves. Sally swooshed at them with the toes of her sneakers, sending the leaves swirling like tiny doves. Katie carefully stepped on the bare patches of sidewalk, keeping her shiny patent leather shoes free of leaf mush. Up ahead the street was jammed with cars disgorging kids with backpacks. The kids ran into the fenced-in playground of Montgomery Elementary School, a three-story brick building with sturdy granite columns flanking its front door. The building had a basketball court on one side and a cluster of crooked pine trees on the other side.

"Okay, you two," said Darlene, finally closing her compact. "Get lost. One of your parents will pick you up after school. Don't know which parent. Don't care." She sauntered off, popping a wad of gum into her mouth. Sally stuck her tongue out at Darlene's retreating back.

"You shouldn't do that," said Katie, gasping in horror. "My Mom says that kids should always show adults the proper respect."

Sally snorted. "Darlene's not an adult. She's a doofus." She skipped around Katie, chanting. "Darlene, Darlene, she's not too keen. She's the biggest dunce you've ever seen."

Katie turned red. She quickly looked around to make sure that Darlene hadn't heard. Darlene was examining her nails as she walked away, completely oblivious to the kids dodging around her on the sidewalk. Katie breathed a sigh of relief and followed Sally into the school building.

"Okay, everyone settle down!" Mr. Zukas' deep voice boomed over the chaos in his fifth-grade classroom. He gave his sweater vest a firm tug and strode to the front of the class. "Get to your desks, pronto. Tommy, get your foot out of Kyle's mouth. Patricia, give Tiffany back her shoes. They're too small for you anyway, you clodhopper."

Thirty kids rushed to their seats with a sound like elephants tap dancing. Sally threw herself into her assigned seat in the front row of desks. Katie lowered herself demurely into the seat directly behind Sally. Arnold the Iguana calmly surveyed the classroom from his cage at the back.

Mr. Zukas opened a fat textbook. As he slowly searched for the page he wanted Sally started to fidget. She squirmed like an eel, sat on her hands, and finally couldn't contain herself any longer. She raised her arm and began waving it furiously back and forth. Mr. Zukas ignored her and turned another page.

Never one to be discouraged, Sally climbed onto her chair and waved both arms wildly like a pint-sized airport worker guiding a jumbo jet into a parking space.

"Sally Jane Hesslop," sighed Mr. Zukas, not looking up, "get down off of there before you break your neck. Not that I would mind, but the principal gets grumpy when students kick the bucket."

"Sorry, Mr. Zukas," said Sally, climbing down. "I just had a question. Can we have more discusses on evolution? Cause I looked it up on Google and a Google person says we came from tadpoles. I think it would be cool to be a tadpole. I had a tadpole once. I kept it in a Sprite bottle. After I drank the Sprite, of course. But then my brother Robbie drank the tadpole. Are we having fish sticks for lunch today?"

Mr. Zukas rubbed his forehead, looked longingly at the clock, and sighed again. "I haven't checked the lunch menu today, Sally. It's posted on the cafeteria door. You can check at recess. And no, we don't come from tadpoles. We are primates, which means we are related to the great apes. Our closest cousins are the chimpanzees. All of which I told you yesterday, and which you'd remember if you'd been paying attention. Now, class, open your history books to page thirty-four. The Pioneers. They crossed the Great Plains in covered wagons. Conditions were harsh. They had to hunt for their food."

A small red-haired boy wearing a shirt and tie waved politely from the desk next to Sally.

"Yes, Rodney?" asked Mr. Zukas. "Did you have a question?"

"Not a question, Mr. Zukas. Just a remark. It might interest the class to know that the Pioneers frequently ate deer as well as buffalo. They shot them with rifles."

Mr. Zukas beamed at him. "That's right, Rodney. I'm glad someone's been doing their homework."

Rodney smirked proudly while behind him the rest of the class rolled their eyes.

"Can anyone else tell me what other animals the Pioneers might have hunted?" asked Mr. Zukas.

Sally waved furiously.

"Anyone at all?" Mr. Zukas asked somewhat desperately.

Sally bounced up and down in her seat, arm still waving.

Mr. Zukas sighed. "Yes, Sally."

"They ate gophers."

Loud expressions of disgust erupted from the rest of the class. Sally turned around and glared at them.

"I'm fairly certain the Pioneers didn't eat gophers, Sally," said Mr. Zukas. "I believe gophers are inedible."

"Nuh-*uh*," said Sally. "Gophers are super edible. The Pioneers roasted them over campfires and put hot sauce on them. They tasted like corn dogs. Only furry."

"Eeeww." The rest of the class unanimously decided it was

grossed out. Rodney cleared his throat and looked disdainfully at Sally.

"In the unlikely event that the Pioneers ate gophers," said Rodney with a sneer, "they would have skinned them first. The fur would have been removed before roasting."

"Nuh-uh," retorted Sally. "The fur's where all the vitamins are. Just like potatoes. You keep the skin on for the vitamins."

Behind Sally, Katie gasped and put her hand over her mouth. She had turned a sickly shade of green.

Mr. Zukas peered at her. "Katie, do you need to use the Little Girl's Room?"

Katie nodded tearfully at him. He waved impatiently in the direction of the door and Katie dashed out of the classroom.

Mr. Zukas sighed and turned a page in his textbook. "Let's get off the topic of the Pioneers' diet. Class, have a look at the picture on the next page. See the tin star this man is wearing? That meant he was a sheriff. He kept order in the lawless Wild West. Of course, it was a difficult job, and he needed lots of help. Frequently he would deputize. That means to create a kind of temporary sheriff. Who do you think he deputized?"

"Hamsters," said Sally at once.

Mr. Zukas pulled at his tie, looking like he was tempted to strangle himself with it. "Hamsters cannot be deputies or anything else in the law enforcement arena, Sally. Hamsters are furry rodents, just like gophers."

Sally's eyes flashed dangerously. "Hamsters are nothing like gophers! Hamsters and gophers are sworn enemies. Just ask my hamster, Melvin. You don't want to get him started on gophers. He gets so mad his fur stands straight up and he hops around like microwave popcorn. Besides, hamsters can *so* be in the law enforcement arena. Melvin is in the law enforcement arena. He's a Secret Agent. He has a Secret Agent JetPack and everything. He straps it on and flies around

San Francisco looking for bad guys. If he finds any bad guys he zaps them with his Secret Agent Laser Gun." Sally jumped up and aimed an imaginary laser gun at Mr. Zukas. "Kerpow!"

Mr. Zukas sighed and put a hand on his forehead. "Recess is early today," he said. "Everyone clear out of here. And stay out until the bell rings. I don't care if a tornado sweeps through the schoolyard. If anyone so much as puts one toe inside this classroom in the next half hour I'll personally feed them to the monster that lives in the school basement. He loves to snack on little kids. Especially ones who own hamsters."

"THERE HE IS. Charlie Sanderson, Snot Extraordinaire. Are you ready?" Sally was on the Jungle Gym, hanging upside down by her knees. One of her braids had come undone and her long hair was covering her face. She parted it with her hands and peered at a blond-haired boy walking past. He was wearing baggy pants, expensive sneakers, and a backwards baseball cap and was surrounded by a bunch of boys dressed exactly like him.

Katie peered up at Sally worriedly from a safe perch on the lowest bar of the Jungle Gym. She had her skirt neatly tucked under her legs and her shiny patent leather shoes were carefully resting on a clean patch of grass. "Ready for what?" she asked.

"The Plan," whispered Sally.

"You never told me the plan. I don't know what to do. You just said you had a Secret Revenge Plan, and that there were no Iguanas."

"That's right," said Sally. "We don't need an Iguana for this plan, which is a good thing because Arnold the Iguana is retiring from the revenge business. Arnold had a little chat with Melvin at one of their Secret Agent meetings in the school cafeteria. Arnold told Melvin that he was getting too old for Secret Revenge Plans. He's going to retire to a home for elderly Iguanas in Florida. They spend all day sleeping in hammocks and drinking chocolate milkshakes. Melvin tried to talk him out of it. Mel's afraid Arnold will get fat from all the chocolate milkshakes, but Arnold's already pretty fat because Emily Niederbacher keeps feeding him her peanut butter and jelly sandwiches." Sally grabbed the Jungle Gym bar with both hands, flipped her legs through and dropped to the ground. "We don't need Arnold for this particular Secret Revenge Plan. You can be my back up. Follow me."

Katie sighed and reluctantly followed Sally across the playground.

Sally swerved around a group of kids playing hopscotch and sauntered in the direction of Charlie Sanderson and his posse, who were leaning against the schoolyard's chain-link fence and attempting to look cool. One of the boys nudged Charlie in the ribs and pointed at Sally.

Sally walked up to Charlie and slapped him on the back. "How's it going, Sanderson?"

The posse laughed and Charlie angrily pushed Sally away. "Get away from me, Hesslop, you freak."

Sally smiled. "I may be a freak, but you're a geek. And may I say, you really reek."

Charlie tried to shove her again, but Sally dodged away. She waved at Charlie as he and his posse stalked off to a far corner of the playground. Sally pulled something out of her pocket and tied it to the chain-link fence.

"What are you doing?" whispered Katie. "Are we going to get in trouble again? I can't go to the Principal's office again. I just can't. Mrs. Finsterman always says she's going to pinch my arm with that clothes pin she keeps on her desk."

"She won't pinch you," said Sally, watching the boys depart.

"How do you know? She always says she will."

"I know 'cause she always says she's going to pinch me too, but she never does. It's a psychotogical strategy, like when Xena pretended to be a goddess and the Mud People worshipped her."

Katie stared at her in bafflement. "Mrs. Finsterman is a Mud Person?"

Sally put a finger to her mouth to shush Katie and pointed at the group of boys. Charlie and his gang were about twenty yards away, torturing a first-grader by throwing pebbles at him. The first-grader hopped around like a frightened puppy, not sure whether to cry or run.

Sally checked the fence and muttered to herself. "Two more feet. Come on, you poophead. Keep walking."

Katie frowned at her in confusion. She peered at the group of boys then bent down to examine the fence. "Sally, what . . ."

Sally waved her arms to shush her. The school bell rang, signaling the end of recess. Kids started running for the doors. Charlie Sanderson and his posse followed at a leisurely pace. Suddenly Charlie halted, frowning. He pulled at the waistline of his baggy pants, shrugged, and took another step. Sally yanked Katie away from the fence, giggling wildly. She ran into the school building, pulling Katie along behind her.

A huge burst of laughter suddenly erupted from the school yard. Sally stood on her tiptoes and peeked out of the glass window in the front door of the building. Charlie Sanderson was standing in the middle of the playground with his baggy pants down around his ankles and his *Finding Nemo* underpants on display for all to see. Kids pointed at him, wetting themselves from laughing. Grinning wickedly, Sally pulled a small piece of fishing line from her pocket and showed it to Katie.

Chapter Three

S ALLY WAS LYING on the floor of the Hesslop's living room, peering under an armchair. Muttering under her breath, she reached under the chair and pulled out a slinky and a blackened banana peel. Behind her, Robbie was sitting in the middle of the room wearing Snoopy underpants and his bike helmet. He giggled and whacked himself on the head with a toilet brush, matching the rhythm of Michael Jackson's *Beat it*, which was playing on the radio.

Sally sighed. The armchair was not delivering the goods. She crawled over to the sofa. Darlene Trockworthy was sitting there with her legs stretched out on the coffee table, painting her toenails. As she crawled under Darlene's legs Sally accidentally bumped them. A streak of Cotton Candy pink shot across Darlene's toes and up her ankle.

"Damn it, kid," groused Darlene, "Watch what you're doing. You made me mess up my pedicure."

"Sorry," Sally mumbled grudgingly. "It's just that I can't find Melvin. Have you seen him?"

"Nope, and good riddance," said Darlene. "That rodent's always creeping around underfoot. I swear he tries to trip me on purpose."

Sally sat back on her heels and smirked at Darlene. "He does that 'cause it's part of his Secret Mission. He's Special Agent Melvin, and he goes to Washington BC every weekend for Super Secret Hamster Orders. He's trained to trip all enemy combatants."

Darlene wiped the nail polish off her foot. "Well, if you can't find him maybe he's at the White House meeting the President," she said. "I hear they serve hamster every Friday."

Sally gave her an evil glare and flopped on her stomach to peer under the sofa.

Behind her Melvin suddenly appeared, rolling across the living room on an old-fashioned four-wheeled roller skate. His chubby rear-end didn't quite fit on the skate, and he dusted a path across the floor with his fur. He rolled from one end of the room to the other and disappeared into the kitchen. Robbie waved the toilet brush at him as he passed.

Sally pulled her head out from under the sofa and hopped to her feet. She planted her fists on her hips. "Drat you, Melvin. Where *are* you? If you're hiding in the microwave again I'm going to spank your little furry butt. You know Dad hates it when his microwave popcorn tastes like hamster."

She stomped into the kitchen and opened the microwave. No Melvin. She banged open cupboards and rattled pans. "Melvin, if you've gone on a Secret Mission again you are soooo in trouble. You know you aren't supposed to go on Secret Missions after your bedtime. I'm gonna write to Washington. They'll remote you back to Janitor Melvin and take away your Secret Agent Jetpack."

Sally crawled under the kitchen table and peered inside an empty box of Wheaties. Behind her Melvin had managed (by methods known only to himself and other Secret Agent Hamsters) to get himself on top of the fridge. He poked his nose over the side and surveyed the perilous drop to the kitchen counter. After a moment's hesitation, he stepped off the fridge, executing a perfect swan dive with a half-twist. He landed face-first on the kitchen counter then slowly toppled over onto his back, legs in the air. He tried to roll onto his feet but was hampered by a touch of middle-aged spread. After several tries he got himself right-side up and waddled to the edge of the countertop. At that moment Robbie wandered in, fencing with his toilet brush. Melvin took a step into the unknown and landed splat on top of Robbie's bike helmet, all four feet splayed out and hanging on for dear life. Oblivious to his stowaway, Robbie fenced back into the living room, taking Melvin with him.

"Sally, get off the floor," said Mr. Hesslop as he entered the kitchen, a pencil behind his ear and the grumpy look of a man who's just been wrestling with his tax returns. "You're as bad as Robbie. Remember, you're supposed to set a good example for him. Now, go brush your teeth. It's bedtime."

Sally scrambled out from under the table and saluted. "Sir. Yes Sir. Your orders we obey. We're here to save the day. Good dental hygiene is a must. We'll clean our teeth or bust." She marched out of the kitchen, humming a martial tune. At the end of the hall she pivoted sharply and entered a small bathroom whose plumbing fixtures dated from the fifties. A bulging hamper full of wet towels sat in the corner and a flotilla of rubber ducks was lined up along the edge of the bathtub. The back of the toilet overflowed with half-empty shampoo bottles.

Sally knelt and began throwing towels out of the hamper. "Melvin, you varmint, you're about to become a garment. My Xena doll needs a fur coat, and you've got my vote."

She stuck her head into the now empty hamper. Behind her Melvin sauntered into the bathroom and scrambled up onto the edge of the tub, climbing the pyramid of wet towels Sally had dumped on the floor. He wound his way along the rim of the bathtub, which was full of soapy water leftover from Robbie's bath. Melvin dodged the rubber ducks with surprising agility, but overconfidence got the better of him and he slipped, falling into the bathtub with a splash.

Sally pulled her head out of the hamper and rushed over. "Melvin, you poophead. Your Secret Agent Swimming Lessons aren't til next week."

A stream of bubbles floating up from under the water was the only answer. Sally scooped Melvin up and deposited him on the bathroom rug. Melvin shook like a tiny dog and sat shivering, his orange fur matted to his sides.

"It's okay, Mel," said Sally. "I'll fix you right up with my Top Secret Air Blaster."

She grabbed a blow drier and turned it on High. The blast of hot air rolled Melvin over backward. He did a full somersault and ended up on standing on his head against the side of the bathtub. Sally picked him up and aimed the blow drier at his tummy. His fur blew straight backward as if he was in a hurricane. When Sally had finished drying him he was twice his normal size and had the hamster version of an Afro.

"Melvin! That's a great disguise. You can use it on your next undercover mission. Nobody will ever recognize you. You can be Horace the Hairdresser, famous for your skills with a curling iron. All the lady hamsters will be lining up to make an appointment with you."

Melvin's Afro started to deflate.

"Hang on Melvin," said Sally. "You just need some Product to maintain volume. That's what those hair commercials on TV are always saying."

Sally grabbed a can of hair mousse from the cabinet under the sink and sprayed a big glob on Melvin, who promptly disappeared under a pile of foam. Sally dug him out of the foam and rubbed the mousse into his fur, then snatched a toothbrush from the sink. "This is Dad's. He won't mind," said Sally as she brushed Melvin's fur into spikes. She sat him back down on the bathroom rug.

"There! You totally look like a cool dude. You look like one of those singers on American Idol. You just need to learn how to dance."

Sally jumped up and launched into a wild dance step. Melvin backed into a corner as Sally's flailing arms whacked the shower curtain and knocked a shampoo bottle into the toilet. Sally finished with a flourish and bowed low before an imaginary audience. "C'mon Mel. It's not hard. You just do little wiggle and a little rap. You just gotta have attitude. Like this."

Sally grabbed a rubber duck and sang into it like a microphone. "My name's Sally J. and I'm here to say, I'm doing my dance 'cause I pulled down Charlie's pants."

Sally picked up Melvin and danced around with him. "You need a hamster rap. All the tough hamsters have one. And maybe some bling. I wonder if Dad would buy you a gold chain."

Melvin looked decidedly skeptical about this, not to mention seasick from all the dancing.

Sally danced into her bedroom, singing. "I'm furry and I'm cute. I'm a Secret Agent to boot. I've got a special JetPack which is totally wack."

She tucked Melvin into his Hamster Habitat. Melvin trundled down the orange tube to his usual nest, his sticky moussed fur attracting bits of sawdust. By the time he reached his nest in the middle of the Habitat he looked like a tiny pile of kindling.

"Another super disguise, Mel," said Sally. "Totally cool. You can do your next Secret Mission at Tony's Pizza. They have sawdust all over their floor. They'll never spot you. You can sneak into the kitchen and find out the ingredients of their Secret Pizza Sauce."

Melvin burrowed into the sawdust of his nest until he was just a sawdust-lump. Sally yawned and blew him a kiss. "Night Mel."

Chapter Four

"**S**ALLY JANE HESSLOP, you are a demon spawn."

Mrs. Patterson, leader of Girl Scout Troop 112, wiped the milk off her sour face and glared down at Sally. The two of them were faced off in the middle of the Montgomery Elementary School cafeteria. A table with cartons of milk and a plate of Rice Krispie Treats was setup in one corner.

The wayward milk had ended up on Mrs. Patterson's face through totally unavoidable circumstances. Sally had been chasing another Girl Scout while holding a carton of milk and a straw. Squirting had been inevitable.

Sally planted her fists on her hips and regaled Mrs. Patterson with a cold stare. They were old enemies. They had disliked each other from the very first day that Mrs. Patterson had assumed the leadership of the troop. On that fateful day Sally had been showing the other Girl Scouts how to slide along the newly polished wooden floor in their stocking feet. She had just launched into a particularly energetic slide when Mrs. Patterson had walked through the door of the cafeteria. The resulting collision had knocked Mrs. Patterson off her feet and onto her support-hose covered knees. Mrs. Patterson had been trying to transfer Sally to another Girl Scout troop ever since, so far without success.

"Well," said Sally, "if I'm a demon spawn then I bet it's a cool demon, one that can shoot flames out of its eyeballs. I wish I could shoot flames out of my eyeballs. I'd turn Charlie Sanderson into a crispy critter."

Mrs. Patterson raised her eyes to the heavens. "When I say that you are a demon spawn, Sally Jane Hesslop, it means that you are a very bad girl. One of the worst I've had the misfortune to meet in all my years of guiding Girl Scouts along the difficult path to becoming young ladies."

Sally fiddled with her straw. "I'd rather be a demon spawn than a young lady. I bet demon spawn have cool super powers. The coolest super power would be to turn people into potato bugs. My first victim would be Charlie Sanderson. If I turned him into a potato bug it would be a big improvement. I'd probably get a medal from the President. Then they'd have a parade for me and I'd ride on a float past the White House and wave to the crowd. Like this." Sally energetically waved her arms, spraying drops of milk onto Mrs. Patterson's bouffant hairdo.

Mrs. Patterson closed her eyes and kneaded her forehead with two shaking fingers. "Sally Jane Hesslop, we were discussing you spewing milk everywhere and making a mess, not super powers and potato bugs. Now go get some paper towels from the restroom and wipe this up."

"Okay" said Sally, shrugging. She tucked the straw under her Girl Scout beanie. "When do we get to make bird feeders from pinecones? That's in the Girl Scout handbook, you know. Page forty-nine. You stick peanut butter in the pinecones so the birds can peck it out. Though I don't understand why we can't just spread the peanut butter on Ritz crackers. Then the birds could peck it real easy. Molly Sanderson says it's because the birds like to work hard for their food, but that's just stupid. Besides, Molly is Charlie Sanderson's sister and she picks her nose, so you know anything she says is suspected. That's what my Dad says. Nose pickers are Dim Bulbs and to be suspected. The crackers don't have to be Ritz. Wheat Thins would work good too."

Mrs. Patterson sighed. "Sally Jane Hesslop, I don't know what you're blathering on about. Get this mess cleaned up. *Now.*"

Mindy Nichols, a thin black girl with red bows on the ends of her cornrows, ran up to Sally. She peered after the departing Mrs. Patterson with a fearful expression. "Sally, guess what? Mrs. Osterman isn't coming today. She's in the hospital."

Mrs. Osterman was the co-leader of the troop. She was a quiet young woman with a warm smile who was liked by all the Girl Scouts.

"You mean it's just us and Prissy Patterson?" groaned Sally. "Oh barf. Why is Mrs. Osterman in the hospital?"

"Molly Sanderson says it's because she's having an *operation,*" whispered Mindy.

Sally rolled her eyes. "Molly is always saying stupid stuff. You know that. She's a Sanderson. You can't believe anything she says. C'mon. Let's go ask Sandra Chang. She'll know."

Sally and Mindy ran up to a group of girls gathered around Sandra Chang, a tall, graceful Chinese girl with a curtain of shiny black hair hanging all the way to her hips. A purple silk scarf was artfully tied around the neck of her Girl Scout uniform.

Sally barged her way through the group. "Hey Sandra."

Sandra nodded at her graciously, like a benevolent Queen acknowledging her subjects.

"Sandra, what's up with Mrs. Osterman? Mindy says she's in the hospital."

"I'm sorry, Sally," replied Sandra Chang in a quiet, authoritative voice. "I don't know the details. All I know is that Mrs. Patterson is taking over as Troop Leader."

Loud groans erupted from all the Girl Scouts within earshot. Molly Sanderson, a short, pudgy blond girl with two front teeth missing, sister to the infamous Charlie Sanderson, jumped up and down frantically, waving her hand as if in school.

"Thandra. Thandra," lisped Molly, "I know what'th happened to Mrs. Othterman. My brother Charlie told me."

On hearing Charlie's name Sally made loud gagging noises and clutched her throat. Molly ignored her, looking intently at Sandra. Finally Sandra gave her a regal nod.

"Mrs. Othterman ith having a Hystertology," whispered Molly excitedly. "That'th an operation. It meanth thee can't have babiesth anymore, unlesth she goeth to Mexico and getsth it reverthed. Then her babiesth will come out backwardsth, like when your Dad backth the car out of the garage. Latht week my Dad backed our car out of the garage and ran over my brother'th bicycle. My Dad said a very bad wordth."

Sally planted her hands on her hips and gave Molly a look of scathing contempt. "That's not a Hystertology, Sanderson. A Hystertology is when you have your ears pinned back. The doctor staples them to your head so you don't look like Dumbo."

"Mrs. Othterman doesthn't look like Dumbo," said Molly.

"Well, not anymore," shot back Sally. "She's had a Hystertology. Sheesh, Sanderson. You are such a dimwit sometimes. I guess it runs in the family."

Molly advanced on her, fists clenched. "You take that back Hessthlop."

Sally assumed a Xena fighting pose. "C'mon, Sanderson. I'll lick you, and then I'll go lick your stupid brother."

"Charlie's a twit,

He's Molly's brother.

He has half a wit,

Molly has the other."

Sally raised her leg in preparation for a super-duper martial arts kick. Molly stood her ground for a second, then thought better of it and dashed off to find Mrs. Patterson.

"Girls! Girls!" shouted Mrs. Patterson from the center of the cafeteria. "Everyone gather round. It's Share Time. Bring the item you're going to share with the group over here."

There was a noisy scramble as all the Girl Scouts rushed to a pile of backpacks stacked against the wall, and then convened in the center of the room. They threw themselves on the wooden floor in a cross-legged circle around Mrs. Patterson.

"Molly, dear, why don't you go first," said Mrs. Patterson.

Molly Sanderson smirked at the others and walked to the center of the circle. She held up a Barbie doll dressed in an immaculate princess-type costume of white silk with a red velvet cape. "Thith ith Princeth Thophie of Bavaria. Thee's dressthed for the ball. Thee's a Spethial Edition. My Mom bought her for me in New York at Bloomingdaleth."

"She's just beautiful, Molly," said Mrs. Patterson. "So precious. I bet all the young ladies here want to be Princesses, don't you, girls?"

Sally sprang up. "Of course. I'm Princess Scary Fighting Eagle from the Moping Moose tribe. We get dressed for balls too. We paint our faces with red stripes, stick eagle feathers in our ears, and do our Special Moose Waltz around the campfire."

Sally launched into a fast-paced dance, shaking her arms and kicking her legs over her head. Her beanie flew off, and girls scrambled backwards as she lunged wildly toward them. She concluded by spinning rapidly in a circle, then staggered dizzily back to her spot on the floor.

Mrs. Patterson closed her eyes during this performance. After Sally had sat down again she opened her eyes, a pained expression on her face. "Mindy," she sighed, "why don't you go next?"

Mindy Nichols moved to the center of the circle, bashfully pulling at her cornrows. She pulled a brightly colored paper bird from a bag. Several of the Girl Scouts oohed and aahed. Mindy smiled gratefully.

"This is a Japanese art called Origami. My Mom learned it when she was stationed at a Navy base in Sasebo, Japan. She taught it to me. This is a tsuru. That's Japanese for crane. All the kids in Japan learn to make them. The crane is a symbol of peace." Mindy sat down abruptly, looking embarrassed. The scouts applauded.

Mrs. Patterson pursed her lips as if she'd just drunk lemon juice. "Very, er, multi-cultural, Mindy. Though maybe you should bring something a little more American next time. These exotic things aren't really appropriate for Girl Scout meetings. Let's see, Sandra, why don't you come up."

Sandra Chang nodded and rose gracefully to her feet. She unrolled a paper scroll which displayed a vertical line of beautiful Chinese characters. "This is called calligraphy. It's a very popular art in China. These characters are in the Mandarin language, which my mother and grandmother speak. My grandmother taught me how to do calligraphy. We use a pot of black ink and a brush made of sheep's hair."

Sandra sat down and the Girl Scouts applauded respectfully.

"My goodness," said Mrs. Patterson, "This is certainly an international group. I feel like I'm at the United Nations. Well, onward. Who'd like to volunteer?"

Sally waved her arm wildly. Another scout across from Sally dared to raise her arm as well. Sally glared daggers at her opponent, and the offending scout promptly dropped her challenge and looked like she'd be thrilled to sink into the floor. Mrs. Patterson tried mightily to avoid Sally's gaze, but resistance was futile. Sally marched unbidden to the center of the circle, carrying a paper takeout carton. Mrs. Patterson raised her eyes heavenward.

"I'll go next, Mrs. Patterson," said Sally. She opened the carton and pulled out something wriggly. The Girl Scouts gasped in horror and the ones closest scooted away. Molly Sanderson screamed.

"Mrsth. Patterthon, Thally'th brought a rat! Eeeuww. Make her take ith away!"

Sally rolled her eyes. "It's not a rat, Sanderson, you doofus. It's my hamster, Melvin. My Dad shaved him. See, what happened was, I put some of Darlene Trockworthy's Super Hold Hair Mousse on him. Darlene wants to be my Dad's girlfriend, and she left her hair mousse in our bathroom."

Mrs. Patterson clutched the pearls around her neck and muttered something about tramps.

"Anyway," continued Sally, "it turns out you should never mousse a hamster. It glues their fur up something awful. Plus you should especially never put mousse on your hamster and then let him roll around in sawdust. My Dad said there must have been some kind of chemical reaction between the pine sap in the sawdust and Darlene's Super Hold Hair Mousse. It hardened up like that shellac stuff we used on our birdhouses last year. Poor Mel here couldn't even walk. He just rolled around like a pinecone with feet. So my Dad used his electric razor and shaved off all of Melvin's fur. So now Mel's got a crew cut, like an Army guy. Anybody want to hold him?"

The scouts all recoiled. Melvin dove back into the takeout container as Mrs. Patterson stepped forward and made shooing motions at Sally. Sally reluctantly relinquished center stage and sat back down. She dropped a Rice Krispie Treat into the takeout carton. "It's okay, Mel," she whispered into the carton, "Don't mind Prissy Patterson. The troop loved you. You were a big hit."

End of Excerpt